Was her *dat* pushing Adrian to date her?

"Adrian, I am mortified."

"Why would you be?" He looked at her quizzically, as if he didn't understand her embarrassment. Then Adrian did something she did not expect. He tipped his hat back and started laughing.

"I fail to see what's so funny."

"Come on, Grace. It's not unusual for Amish parents to push their single children into dating. You're aware of that I'm sure."

"My parents haven't even mentioned that they think I should date."

"Maybe they're giving you time because of Nicole."

"About that…"

"But any man would be blessed to have you for a *fraa*, Grace. As for Nicole…she's a sweet thing. You shouldn't let your decision to raise your cousin's child keep you from dating."

Except Nicole wasn't her cousin's child. And Grace wasn't sure if now was the time or place to share that fact with Adrian…

Vannetta Chapman has published over one hundred articles in Christian family magazines and received over two dozen awards from Romance Writers of America chapter groups. She discovered her love for the Amish while researching her grandfather's birthplace of Albion, Pennsylvania. Her first novel, *A Simple Amish Christmas*, quickly became a bestseller. Chapman lives in Texas Hill Country with her husband.

Visit the Author Profile page at Harlequin.com.

The Baby
Next Door

Vannetta Chapman

LOVE INSPIRED
INSPIRATIONAL ROMANCE

LOVE INSPIRED®
INSPIRATIONAL ROMANCE

Recycling programs for this product may not exist in your area.

ISBN-13: 978-1-335-48877-0

The Baby Next Door

Copyright © 2021 by Vannetta Chapman

This edition published by arrangement with Harlequin Books S.A.

For questions and comments about the quality of this book, please contact us at CustomerService@Harlequin.com.

Love Inspired
22 Adelaide St. West, 40th Floor
Toronto, Ontario M5H 4E3, Canada
www.Harlequin.com

Printed in U.S.A.

"Finally, brethren, whatsoever things are true, whatsoever things are honest, whatsoever things are just, whatsoever things are pure, whatsoever things are lovely, whatsoever things are of good report; if there be any virtue, and if there be any praise, think on these things."
—*Philippians* 4:8

"If you reveal your secrets to the wind, you should not blame the wind for revealing them to the trees."
—Khalil Gibran

This book is dedicated to Tracy Luscombe,
who loves a good book every bit as much as I do.

Chapter One

Goshen, Indiana, was a beautiful place to be in April, but when Grace Troyer glanced out the kitchen window into the eyes of a llama she fought the urge to scream. She wasn't afraid of llamas, but this particular one tended to spit, and it belonged next door, not on her parents' property. Unfortunately, baby Nicole saw the llama at the same time that Grace did. Nicole wasn't particular as to what animal she was petting. She simply called out, "Mine!" and insisted on moving closer.

"*Nein*, baby girl. That is Adrian's llama, and hopefully he will fetch it soon."

"Problem?" Her *mamm* walked into the room, carrying her knitting basket.

Leslie Troyer carried knitting with her wherever she went. "If we're sitting, we're knitting" was her favorite slogan. It should be cross-stitched and hung on the wall, right beside the Golden Rule.

"*Ya*. The problem is Adrian's llama." The beast was nearly six feet tall, with white-and-brown fleece. He was surprisingly fast, much too curious and had a disconcerting way of staring directly into your eyes without blinking.

"It's an odd-looking animal, for sure and certain."

"Mine, *Mamm*. Mine." Nicole struggled to be let down, so Grace put her on the floor.

Only fourteen months old, she had begun pulling up and clinging to things. Grabbing hold of her mother's dress, Nicole looked up, grinned, then plopped on her bottom, executed a quick change of position to all fours and took off toward the front door.

"She'll be walking soon."

"So you keep warning me."

"After that, your life will never be the same."

In Grace's opinion, they'd already passed that point, but no use bringing it up on a beautiful April morning. Instead, she finished rinsing the last of the breakfast dishes, dried her hands and hurried after her daughter.

She walked into the sitting room to find Nicole had pulled herself up to the glass storm door and was high-fiving none other than Adrian Schrock. He'd squatted down so that their heights matched better. Nicole was having a fine old time. She considered Adrian a top-notch playmate.

Grace picked up her *doschder* and pushed open the door, causing Adrian to jump up, then take a step back toward the porch steps. It was, indeed, a fine spring day. The sun shone brightly across the Indiana fields. Flowers colored yellow, red, lavender and even orange had begun popping through the soil that surrounded the porch. Birds were even chirping merrily.

Somehow, all those things did little to elevate Grace's mood. Neither did the sight of her neighbor.

Aaron resettled his straw hat on his head and smiled. *"Gudemariye."*

"Your llama has escaped again."

"Kendrick? *Ya.* I've come to fetch him. He seems to like your place more than mine."

"I don't want that animal over here, Adrian. He spits."

"We're working on that."

"And your peacock was here at daybreak, crying like a child."

"George Eliot said that animals make agreeable friends because 'they ask no questions' and 'pass no criticisms' or something like that. I'm paraphrasing."

"George Eliot?"

"British author. Nineteenth century."

"Yes, I remember reading her in school." Probably the reason that Grace remembered the author was because Eliot was a woman writing under a man's pen name. "But back to my point—I'd like you to try harder to keep your animals on *your* side of the fence."

Instead of responding to her perturbed tone, Adrian laughed. "When you moved back home, I guess you didn't expect to live next to a Plain & Simple Exotic Animal Farm."

Grace could practically hear the capital letters for Adrian's newest name for his farm. She'd yet to see an official sign by the road. No doubt that would be next, attracting even more *Englischers*. Adrian wiggled his eyebrows at Nicole and was in the middle of yet another laugh when he seemed to realize that Grace wasn't amused. She hated to be a wet blanket, but his animals were driving her slightly batty.

"I think of your place as Adrian's Zoo."

"Not a bad name, but it doesn't highlight our Amish heritage enough."

"The point is that I feel like we're living next door to a menagerie of animals."

"Remember when we went to the zoo over in South Bend? When was that, fourth grade? That was quite the trip."

That was part of their problem—she and Adrian shared a history together. To be more precise, they'd attended the same school and church meetings. He'd been two grades ahead of her. They'd never been what you might call close. If he'd been a stranger, she might have been able to be more firm, more brusque. As it was, there was an uneasy familiarity between them that forced her to be polite.

As for the zoo trip, Grace remembered monkeys that screeched and the reptile house that Eli Zook had taken her to, insisting she'd love it. She didn't love it. And when she'd screamed upon seeing the giant boa constrictor, Eli had laughed until he was bent over. Although she'd thought she had a crush on Eli, she'd known he wasn't the one for her at that very moment.

Thirteen years later, and she still hadn't found the one—though, of course, she'd thought she had with Nicole's father. That was a mental path she didn't want to go down this morning. But looking at Adrian, she remembered Eli and it occurred to her that the two should be best friends. They certainly shared similar interests.

"What ever happened to Eli Zook?"

"Eli?"

Nicole had crawled over to Adrian and had pulled up to a standing position by clinging to his pants leg.

"Eli moved to Florida. He operates a gator farm there,

close to Sarasota. Lots of Amish, but *Englischers* come by, as well."

"You two are not normal Amish men."

"Normal is underrated. Isn't it?"

"Up, Aden. Up."

Adrian scooped her up, held her high above his head, then nuzzled her neck. He treated her like one of his pets. Adrian was comfortable with everyone and everything.

"Do you think she'll ever learn to say my name right?"

"Possibly. Can you please catch Kendrick and take him back to your place?"

"Of course. That's why I came over. I was feeding the turtles, and next thing I knew, Kendrick was hightailing it down my lane. I guess I must have left the gate open again." He kissed Nicole's cheek, then popped her back into Grace's arms. "You should bring baby girl over to see the turtles. They like to sun out on the log in the middle of the pond—anytime after noon."

"We have a pretty busy day planned." Her only plans were laundry and cleaning, but it seemed rude to say that she didn't want to visit his place—between the llamas, emus and wild birds, the place creeped her out a little bit.

As he walked away, Grace wondered for the hundredth time why he wasn't married. It was true that he'd picked a strange profession. She didn't know of a single other Amish man who raised exotic animals. How did that even produce an income to live on? No, Adrian wouldn't be considered excellent marrying material by most young Amish women.

But on the other hand he was fairly young—twenty-five years to her twenty-three. He also looked like the typical Amish male who romance authors wrote about and young Amish women dreamed of—brown hair cut as if a bowl had been placed over his head, eyes the color of caramel and an easy smile.

He was good-looking, if you went for the tall, thin type, which she didn't. Grace was suspicious of people who were too thin. She always felt the urge to feed them.

She hadn't been thin even before Nicole was born, and the baby weight she'd gained during pregnancy hadn't disappeared after Nicole's birth. It didn't matter, she told herself as she carried Nicole back inside. She felt healthy, and she wasn't in the market for a man. If she was, and weight kept them apart, then he was not the kind of man she would want.

What was she talking about?

A man was the reason she was in this situation to begin with. She shook away the memories, again making a mental effort not to dwell on the past this fine day.

"Let's go change the sheets."

In response, Nicole put her head on Grace's shoulder and popped the two forefingers of her right hand into her mouth. As Grace walked up the stairs, she glanced out the living room window in time to see Adrian leading Kendrick the Llama back to his property.

They were the same height. As she watched, Adrian took the hat off his head and set it on the llama, who tolerated such silliness for all of a dozen steps before casting it off. She could practically hear Adrian's laugh from where she stood. Well, she couldn't hear it but she could imagine it. He was a lighthearted fellow, but then his life had been relatively easy. Why wouldn't he be carefree? He hadn't made the kinds of life-altering mistakes that she had.

Only Grace couldn't quite bring herself to think of Nicole as a mistake. She hadn't realized it was possible to love someone so much that your heart literally ached, but when she'd first held her newborn daughter, she'd felt that exact thing—a yearning and satisfaction that seemed to exist at the same time but in tension with one another.

Her life had definitely changed in the eighteen months she'd been effectively exiled to her *aenti*'s home in Ohio. She'd grown up, learned what responsibility really was and abandoned any ideas of a *rumspringa*. She'd become a mother and a woman, putting childish things aside.

She'd returned home to find that her parents' home and the small town of Goshen were much the same as before she'd left. The only dramatic change had been at the property next door. No one had lived on the place as long as she could remember—though when she was a child, someone had leased it and worked the fields. But the fields had lain fallow for a long time.

There wasn't even a house there.

As a child, Grace and her siblings had run through the pastures enjoying games of tag.

She'd been surprised to learn that Adrian had bought the property and begun building his exotic-animal zoo. Since they were outside Goshen city limits, there were no restrictions on what animals he could and couldn't own. She certainly hoped he'd stay away from reptiles. Perhaps she should talk to him about that.

Regardless of Adrian's plans, which were really none of her business, she was glad to be back in Indiana, in Goshen and in their Plain community.

She was grateful that her parents had allowed her to come home. Grace had realized while staying with her *aenti* in her rather large Mennonite community that she wanted to be Plain, and she wanted to raise Nicole that way. If it meant confessing all of her misdeeds in order to live in Goshen, then she was willing to do exactly that.

The strange thing was that, so far, there had been no one to make a confession to.

She was both relieved and perplexed.

She'd tried a few times to start a conversation with her old school friends—who had quickly changed the subject. Her oldest *schweschdern* had been the one to tell her that people thought Nicole belonged to their cousin in Ohio and that Grace had agreed to raise her. Grace didn't know where they'd come up with that idea, but then again, it was somewhat common for Amish families to take in an extra child or two. It was a bit on the unusual side for a single Amish woman to do so.

It seemed people wanted to believe this alternate truth.

Who was she kidding? It wasn't the truth. It was a lie, whether she'd been the one to tell it or not. She needed to set people straight, but how was she to do that other than taking out an ad in the *Goshen Daily News* or the *Budget*?

She planned to join their church in the fall. In fact, the day before, she'd begun attending the class for new members. Bishop Luke instructed the candidates while the rest of the congregation was singing. They'd have nine meetings total. Grace was by far the oldest in the class. Each week, they would cover two different articles of instruction. Luke had led them through Bible verses explaining what it meant to have faith in God as well as the creation story.

Grace wasn't sure exactly what was coming up in the next meetings, but she hoped to have a chance to share the truth of Nicole's parentage.

While she dreaded doing so, another part of her looked

forward to it. She was ready to wipe the slate clean and move on with her life—hers and Nicole's.

If only this could be their life.

If only Nicole's father wouldn't look for her, wouldn't find her.

If only she could relax and feel at home again here in Goshen.

She'd give almost anything for those things to be true. There were days when her mood plummeted, and she thought the heaviness of her sins would pin her to the mattress. She certainly couldn't bring herself to dream of a home and marriage anymore. Those thoughts were like splinters in her heart. *Nein*, she would set her sights lower—a safe home for Nicole, a *gut* place to raise her child, the love and companionship of family. Certainly those things could satisfy the longing in her heart. She was even willing to live next door to the Plain & Simple Exotic Animal Farm, though she certainly wished the owner would keep the animals on his side of the fence.

Adrian whistled all the way home, thinking of the image of Grace and Nicole standing on the front porch. Grace was a nice-looking woman. She had pretty brown eyes that reminded him of freshly baked brownies and blond hair that was exactly the same tint as Kendrick's fur. He didn't understand why she wasn't dating. She'd been back in Goshen for two months. That was enough time to settle back into her parents' home again. The fact that she'd brought Nicole home to raise, well, that just raised her attractiveness in his point of view.

Raising someone else's child, even another relative's, showed she was kind and compassionate.

He'd like to meet a woman like that.

Of course it would have to be a woman who shared his love of animals and nature. Maybe someone who had a bit of a sense of humor. His *mamm* had told him just the other day that "a wife will make or break a household." She was always dropping little proverbs here and there, hoping he'd take the hint.

But Adrian didn't need prodding. He was more than willing to court. The problem was that none of the women he knew seemed willing. True, most were married already. Or too young. The few that were of the right age and single weren't interested in a man who was trying to make a living raising exotic animals.

But it was what he loved, and he felt strongly that God had given him a passion for animals for a reason.

Even though the women in his district couldn't see that.

And Grace Troyer certainly couldn't.

It was a pity, too, because he wouldn't mind courting Grace—except she seemed to have lost her sense of humor and she certainly disliked his "zoo," as she called it.

Back at his place, he tended to his animals and brushed down the emus. It was midafternoon by the time he headed into town. He needed to pick up some supplies, but his real purpose for going was to stop by and see his friend. George Miller was ten years older than Adrian. He had six children, a wife whose quilts were in high demand and a nice seventy-two-acre farm.

Adrian could tell from the boisterous shouts of children coming from behind the house that George was working on the family garden.

"Little early in the year for tilling."

"Tell my *fraa* that. She's already started the cabbage

seeds inside. Says we need to get them in the ground soon."

"I told you not to add that window box to the mud room. It only means extra work for you."

"And yet *gut* food for the table."

"All these rows can't be for cabbage."

"*Nein*—cucumbers, green beans, peppers, tomatoes and potatoes will be added after the cabbage. You know how it is. We're always planting something." George stretched his back until he heard a satisfying pop. "If you came to chat, why don't you help me out while we talk?"

Adrian picked up a hoe and set to work on the next row.

Two of George's oldest children seemed to have the right idea—one was turning over sod and the other was breaking it up. Two others were sitting on the ground, filling pails with dirt, then dumping it back out on their laps. He supposed the youngest two were inside. He felt a prickle of envy and pushed it away. He'd have a family when God was ready for him to have a family. There was no point in worrying over it.

"What are you chewing on over there?"

"Me?"

"You've been standing in the same place since you picked up the hoe."

"Oh. *Ya.*" Adrian focused on moving down the row, matching George's pace. Keeping his hands busy made it easier to share what was weighing on his mind. "I wanted to speak to you about something…about my farm."

"Uh-huh. It's in a nice area—good dirt and tidy farms."

"I want to start a tour out that way."

"I believe you've mentioned as much before." George

kept his attention on the ground, but Adrian knew he was grinning. They'd been friends for many years, and they'd had this discussion several times in the last six months.

"Since you're the head of the Goshen Tourism Board…"

"Goshen Plain Tourism Committee—we're simply a branch of the overall tourism board."

"Whatever. When can we start tours to my place?"

George leaned on his hoe and tipped his hat up. "How many animals do you have now?"

"Two llamas, four alpacas, a couple emus, six exotic birds, some rabbits and goats, which aren't exotic but children love to pet them. Plus the turtles and my three-legged dog."

George signaled for him to keep going.

"Half a dozen wild turkeys, and I'm talking to Simon over in Middlebury about purchasing a camel or two."

"Sounds like things are really progressing."

"They are. I've also set up small pens for a petting area."

"I don't think it's enough."

"I could order a bison or a yak."

George shook his head. "You don't need more animals, or maybe you do—I don't know about that. What I'm saying is that you need other stops on your tour."

That was not what Adrian wanted to hear. He'd spoken to his parents and his *schweschdern*. None of them wanted anything to do with a tour business.

"What would you suggest?"

"A place where guests could purchase handmade items."

"Quilts and such?"

"Sure. *Englischers* believe that all Amish women quilt."

"Your wife certainly does. Maybe she would—"

George held up his hand to stop him. "Becca's willing to provide quilts, but there's no room here to show them. You're going to have to find at least two more stops for your tour."

"Old Saul said he'd be willing to show his dairy cows."

"Gut."

"But my family isn't interested."

"You need a stop where they can eat." George again leaned on his hoe. "Have you tried talking to Grace Troyer?"

"She is *definitely* not interested."

"Have you talked to her parents?"

"Why would I do that?"

George used the edge of the hoe to scoop dirt to the top of the row in front of him. "Grace has been a bit reclusive since she's returned home."

"I wouldn't call her *reclusive*."

"But Leslie and James are much more practical. In fact, if I remember right, Leslie does quite a bit of knitting."

"She does. There are baskets of yarn everywhere."

"And Grace is a *gut* cook, right?"

"She told me once she wanted to go to cooking school."

"An Amish chef?"

"Ya. That was when we were kids." He broke up a particularly big clod of dirt. "You're right that she's been different since she's been back. I think it's because of Nicole. It's a big responsibility to take on, raising someone else's child."

George's head jerked up. He studied Adrian, then shook his head as if to dismiss some idea. "She's an excellent cook, and I know for a fact that her parents can use the money. Talk to them. Maybe they can change her mind."

Adrian didn't think anything would change Grace's mind. She'd once been an outgoing, friendly young woman, but she'd changed. Adrian didn't know what had happened while she was away, but he did know that she wasn't interested in helping him create a successful tour business. What Grace wanted more than anything was to be left alone, and an Amish tour stop would be the exact opposite of that.

Looking in her direction for help was bound to be futile.

His heart sank as he thought of his animals and how much it would cost to feed them over the next year. He needed to make some money, and he did not want to go back to work at the nearby RV factory to do that. He wanted to be on his farm with his animals. If that meant confronting Grace Troyer, then that was what he'd have to do.

He could very well lose the farm if he didn't find a way to raise some money. There were annual taxes to pay, not to mention he needed money for his own food and clothing. Then there was the care of his buggy horse, plus the cost of the animals' feed and the occasional veterinary bill. He also had a responsibility to give to the church.

Adrian needed the tours to happen, and he needed them to happen soon. There was simply no way he was going to let Grace stand between him and his dream.

Chapter Two

The next afternoon Grace found Adrian in the enclosed area that was labeled Exotic Birds Aviary. The structure was approximately fifteen feet wide, twelve feet tall and stretched for the length of most Amish homes. It reminded Grace of a large dog run. The walls and roof were made of chicken fencing, which she supposed kept the birds inside. When she'd first arrived home in February, she'd noticed that Adrian had wrapped the entire thing in plastic sheeting. When she asked him, he said it was so that the plants—and the birds—would stay warm. He'd even set up a heating system that used solar panels.

The plastic had since been removed, bright April sunshine was streaming through the fencing, and the smell of spring was in the air.

Grace had read about aviaries before, and she'd always imagined them as being calm, quiet, peaceful places. Adrian's aviary could best be described as chaotic. The birds set to screeching as soon as she walked inside, a three-legged dog bounded past her and several rabbits hopped toward patches of grass.

"Grace, I'm surprised to see you here." Adrian hurried toward her. "Why are you carrying that rolling pin?"

Grace glanced down at her hand. Why *was* she carrying a rolling pin? Well, that was Adrian's fault. He was the reason she wasn't still rolling out pie crusts. "I'm not here for chitchat, Adrian. Why did you talk my parents into being a stop on your tour?"

"Well, now, I saw your *dat* out in the field early this morning and we got to talking. One thing led to another, and I suppose I mentioned that I could use his help."

"You could use his help?"

"Plus, I thought it might be *gut* for them—financially." A rather large yellow-and-green bird landed on his left shoulder, and Adrian jerked his head to the right, as if to give it more space.

"What is that?"

"This? It's a bird."

"I've never seen one like it before." She realized her tone sounded quite accusatory. Well, it was his fault this bird was here, that this entire menagerie of animals was here and that her parents were buying into his absurd tourist plan. She attempted to refocus on her anger, but the bird was making it difficult. It had begun tweeting quite adamantly.

"You probably haven't seen one like it before because it's from Australia."

"You've been to Australia?"

"*Nein*. A woman in Middlebury bought this one as a pet. She had it for nearly four years. Then a few months ago, she moved into an assisted living facility. She couldn't take the bird with her, so she gave it to me."

"Yes, well—"

"They cost nearly four hundred dollars, so I was quite happy to provide her a home."

"That's *wunderbaar*, but—"

"She's a red-rumped parrot."

That stopped Grace in her tracks. "But she's yellow and turquoise."

Adrian side stepped over to what must have been a feeding station. Grace could just make out scraps of fruit and vegetables scattered across it.

"Dolly has red feathers on her back—all red-rumped parrots do."

As if to show off her best feature, Dolly hopped to the feeding station, turned and walked across the platform. Her colors really were quite exquisite, including bright red feathers on her back. Grace was temporarily speechless.

"Why are you holding a rolling pin?"

She looked at Adrian, then Dolly, then the rolling pin.

"Oh, yes. Well, I was baking, but then Mamm mentioned your tour. So I decided I needed to speak to you about it right away. What were you thinking?" She waved the pin in the air. "Why do you have to drag us into your crazy plans?"

"There was no dragging."

"I'm not interested."

"Apparently your parents are."

"That's beside the point." She slapped the pin against her palm as Adrian added a bit of birdseed to the feeding platform. "Are you even listening to me? I don't want my family involved. I don't want Nicole around all those… strangers."

It sounded lame, even to her own ears, but it was the best explanation she could offer at the moment.

Adrian rubbed his chin thoughtfully as he walked over to a giant birdcage full of finches. The cage reached from the floor to the ceiling, was big enough around that she could have stepped into it and was filled with some sort of shrubbery. Only as she stepped closer, she could see it wasn't all shrubbery—there were dozens of finches inside.

Adrian scooped small black birdseed out of a barrel and deposited it into a feeding tube. "Did you know the size of finches range from four to ten inches?"

Grace held up a hand to stop him. She did not need a lecture on finches. "Adrian, I don't want *Englischers* stomping all over our home."

"Well, we're starting in a week, so it'll probably be warm enough to feed them outside."

"That's another thing… Who decided that I would be willing to cook for twenty people?"

"I thought you liked cooking."

She stared down at the rolling pin. Why couldn't she be home rolling out pie crust? Why did she have to have this conversation? "I do like cooking."

"Then, what's the problem?" He stepped closer, and she had the absurd notion that he meant to reach out and touch her. She stepped back and nearly tripped over a large brown rabbit.

"It's hard to explain. You're going to have to take my word for it."

"Oh." Adrian put both hands on his hips and stared at the ground. Kendrick the Llama walked by the aviary, and Adrian glanced up, then whistled. The beast turned to look at him and immediately took off running in the opposite direction.

Instead of being irritated, Adrian smiled as if a small

child had accomplished a wonderful feat. "What were we talking about?"

"Tours. *Englischers*. Cooking."

"Right. Well, I suppose if you don't want to do it, I could ask Widow Schwartz."

"Are you kidding me? Did you try one of her biscuits last week? *Nein*. You didn't. I know you didn't, because you appear to still have all your teeth."

Adrian started to laugh, but he stopped himself when he caught the frustrated expression on her face.

"I'm sorry, Grace. I—I… Honestly, I thought you enjoyed cooking."

Grace sighed and shifted her weight from one foot to the other.

An owl flew from the back of the aviary to the front and settled on a dead tree limb Adrian had propped against the fence. "Mac had an injured wing. I found him in the barn loft. I think he'll be ready to fly soon." The owl studiously ignored them, tucking its head under its wing.

"I do enjoy cooking."

"So why are you dead set against this?" Adrian stepped closer, stuck his hands in his pockets and waited.

Adrian was comfortable with conversations filled with long pauses. He made her crazy with his animals and his rescues and his short attention span, but she understood that he was a decent person at heart. It was just that his life seemed so chaotic, and by proximity, it seemed to bring disorder and confusion into her life, as well. The one thing Grace didn't need was chaos. She wanted order and quiet and seclusion.

A tourist group didn't bring with it any of those things.

And she was convinced strangers meant danger for Nicole.

She should have never watched that TV show at her *aenti*'s—it was all about what lengths an advocacy group would go to in order to reunite biological dads with their children, even children the fathers hadn't known about.

She'd tried to contact Kolby once, but she'd reached a dead end when the phone number he'd given her no longer worked. Something told her she probably should have tried harder to find him—perhaps legally she was required to try harder.

Grace suddenly felt immensely weary. It was something that happened on a disturbingly regular basis since she'd had Nicole. Most of the time she was fine, then other times she simply wanted to crawl back into bed and sleep for a week.

"Are you okay?"

"I will be." She made no attempt to hide her grimace. "I'm not happy about this, Adrian. I wish you'd asked me first."

"You would have said no."

"Which is exactly my point."

He motioned toward a bench set back in the corner, under an arch that had a flowering vine of some sort growing on it. She hesitated, then took a seat. Adrian leaned against the owl's dead tree limb, arms and ankles crossed, patiently waiting. When she still didn't speak, he hopped in.

"The truth is that I need the tour group. It costs money to feed all of these animals, and then there's the occasional trip to the veterinarian. Plus I have taxes to pay on this place."

"Surely none of that is a surprise."

"It's not, but in my mind if I did the right thing, if I provided a safe habitat for all these animals, then *Gotte* would provide my needs."

"'My God will supply all your needs.' That's Bishop Luke's favorite verse."

"One of them."

"Life isn't that simple, Adrian."

"What do you mean? Give me an example." His attention was completely on her now—something that was rare and disconcerting.

"I know the Bible says that, and I believe it…"

"But?"

"But you also have to use the brain that *Gotte* gave you. Did you work out a business plan at all when you bought the property? You purchased it while I was away, so I had no idea that I would come home to…this. What were you thinking?"

"Oh, I thought about it quite extensively before making an offer. I examined the property closely and did a lot of reading on animal habitat. This place was a real jewel. No home on the property that took up prime animal space—just the barn, which I needed anyway. More importantly, there's a stream and a pond. I knew there would be plenty of water and that I'd have room to grow some of the food."

"Did you think of where you'd live?"

"I live in the barn."

"I'm aware. But certainly you didn't plan to live in a barn. It just happened, right?"

"Now that you mention it, *ya*. It did. I'd planned to stay with my parents a few more years until my business was established. But there's too much work with the animals. They need me morning, noon and night. The travelling back and forth didn't make sense. So I bought a cot and walled off a small area of the barn."

"That's what I'm talking about. You have to think things through. Otherwise you end up sleeping on a cot in the corner of a decrepit barn."

"I suppose, but in my mind, it's also a balance between thinking and trusting." Two rabbits hopped closer, and he pulled a small carrot from each pocket, squatted down and held the offering out in the flat of his palm.

To Grace's surprise, both rabbits hopped forward and took the carrots from him.

"They trust you."

"They do. And I try to trust *Gotte* in the same way."

Grace couldn't resist rolling her eyes. He sounded like a child. Trust was all *gut* and fine until the baby needed diapers or new clothes or a visit to the doctor.

"Can you tell me what—exactly—bothers you about having a tour group here?"

Adrian's question was like a knife twisting in her heart. How could she explain her fear that Nicole's father would turn up one day? She'd first have to explain that Nicole was her *doschder*, and now wasn't the time for that. She had pie shells to roll out and bake.

"*Nein.* I can't."

"Okay." He said the word slowly, as if he didn't understand. Of course he didn't. How could he?

"When my parents agreed to your plan, they didn't realize what they were getting into."

"They're adults, Grace. I'm sure they understood."

"Mamm's all atwitter about having a way to sell her knitted things."

"Which is *gut*, right?"

"As if she didn't have enough projects going. I think her yarn supply is multiplying, like some sort of fungus."

"Your *dat* liked the idea of a tour group, too. He said you all could use the money."

Grace waved that comment away. Her *dat* didn't fully understand the situation. He didn't even know who Nicole's father was. That might sound strange to some people, but in Amish homes, things were often left unsaid. He'd told her that he loved her and would pray for her and the baby, then he'd promptly shipped her off to Holmes County in Ohio—a virtual mecca of Amish and Mennonite.

Only Grace didn't want to live in Ohio.

She wanted to live and raise her child here.

And she didn't want to do it next to a wildlife farm or in the midst of a tour group.

"We've already sold out our first tour—it's next Tuesday."

Grace pinched the bridge of her nose and squeezed her eyes shut. When she opened them, Adrian was still there, still watching her, still waiting.

"I will cook for your group next week, but I want you to try and find someone else, and I don't mean Widow Schwartz. Try to find someone that won't scare your guests away. Maybe…maybe someone would be willing to come here and cook?"

Even as she said it, she knew the odds were slim. From what she'd heard, Adrian didn't even have a kitchen. He had a two-burner stove and a half-size refrigerator.

Adrian assured her he'd keep asking around, then he thanked her for agreeing to help. He wasn't just mouthing the words, either. That was one thing she knew about

Adrian Schrock—he was genuine and always said what was in his heart.

He really was grateful.

Which didn't alleviate her fears about having Nicole around *Englischers* one bit. Well, if Adrian couldn't see her side of things, then she would find ways to encourage him to look elsewhere for a cook.

Maybe her cooking wasn't as good as he thought it was.

Adrian managed to add a camel to his menagerie before the first tour date. The female he purchased was a dromedary, meaning it had only one hump. Simon Lapp in Middlebury had purchased the animal to sell the milk, but after three years, he'd decided it wasn't a cost-effective venture.

"It should have been profitable," he lamented. "Camel milk sells for forty dollars a quart."

Adrian let out a long, low whistle as visions of a fat bank account and the funds to buy more animals popped into his head. "I didn't realize it was worth so much. Why?"

"People with Crohn's disease or diabetes seem to digest it well. That's why I got into the business in the first place. One of my *fraa*'s cousins was having trouble—she has Crohn's disease."

"I'm sorry to hear that, Saul."

"The thing is, no matter how I try, I still can't make a profit."

Adrian's vision of more animals popped like a child's balloon. "Oh."

"The beasts aren't easy to milk, either... Their milk will only let down if the calf is in the next pen, and even then, it only lasts three to four months. Then it's necessary to impregnate the female again."

"So you're out of the camel business?"

"Officially, if you'll take this one."

"What will you do?"

"I'm going back to goats."

Saul hadn't given the camel a name. Adrian couldn't imagine how a person could own an animal for three years without naming it. He immediately named the camel Cinnamon, then ordered a large load of sand to be delivered to his place. He'd already researched the animal's nutritional needs, and he had plenty of hay, which the books recommended, plus small quantities of alfalfa. He wouldn't need to build a hut for shelter until the following winter.

Unfortunately, once delivered to his place Cinnamon wasn't sure about her new digs. She stood in the corner of the fenced area where Adrian had the sand dumped and refused to come close when Adrian called to her. For the first tour, the visitors would have to view her from a distance.

Adrian rose early Tuesday morning and spent most of the day cleaning out pens and making sure the place looked in tip-top shape. Unfortunately, Kendrick escaped again, and he spent an hour locating the llama. He found him half a mile down the road and had to walk him back home. By the time Adrian got back to his place, he barely had time to feed everyone before the tour guests were due to arrive.

He rushed into his home, which was basically a single room on one end of the barn. There was no time for a shower, so instead, he washed up at the kitchen sink and changed into clean clothes. There were twenty people signed up when he'd checked with George, who had arranged transportation from three of the local families. By the time Adrian stepped back outside, Triangle, the cattle dog, was running in a circle and yipping as the buggies pulled up to his gate.

Adrian hurried over and opened the gate, making sure that none of his animals escaped.

The *Englischers* who stepped out of the buggy were wide-eyed and all ears. They'd already been over to Old Saul's, so they'd had a peek at Amish life. Now Adrian was shattering all of those expectations—he was a bachelor, living alone in a barn, raising exotic animals. They'd never heard of such a thing.

He briefly explained that he'd purchased the property a little over a year ago, and he currently had one camel, two llamas, two emus, four alpacas, six exotic birds, rabbits, goats, six wild turkeys and turtles.

"Plus a three-legged dog." A gray-haired man knelt to hold his hand out to the dog.

"That would be Triangle. The vet says he's part cattle dog, and he sort of found me."

"How did a dog happen to find you?" an older woman asked.

"Just showed up, and I couldn't send him away."

"Sounds like my husband—our place looks a little like yours." The man with her immediately started laughing and reaching for his phone to show pictures of their newest rooster.

"You live in the barn?" This came from an older *Englisch* woman who wore a T-shirt that said What Happens with Nana, Stays with Nana.

"*Ya*, though that's only temporary."

"How do you make money off your animals?" an elderly man asked.

"Well, that's why you're here. The price you paid to enjoy this tour helps to purchase the animals' food."

"So why do you do it, if not to make a living?"

"Hopefully one day that will happen. Until then…" Adrian shrugged.

"At least you're not tied to a time clock. That's something to be grateful for, even if you don't have much money."

"Henry David Thoreau agrees with you." When the man looked at him in surprise, Adrian quoted, "I am grateful for what I am and have. My thanksgiving is perpetual."

"Thoreau said that?" The old gent shook his head but smiled. "I've been on Amish tours in Ohio and Pennsylvania…never heard a Plain person quote Thoreau before."

Adrian laughed with them, then invited the guests to stroll around his property and enjoy themselves. "Kendrick the Llama may spit, but he won't bite," he added.

The guests wandered off, chatting and pointing at various animals. Adrian walked over to Seth, who was one of the drivers.

"*Gut* group."

"*Ya.* Thought the old guy was going to drop his teeth when you quoted Thoreau."

"How did it go at Old Saul's?"

"Fine, I suppose. Can't imagine why anyone would want to walk around and look at dairy cows."

"But that's not what they're looking at." Adrian glanced around the farm, taking in the animals and the guests, and smiled in satisfaction. "They're looking at a different life, a life probably very unlike the one they live, and many of them… They're looking into the past, maybe the way their parents or grandparents lived."

He wanted to ask if Seth had talked to Grace or her parents, but Kendrick was stalking the *Englisch* woman wearing a large floppy hat. Adrian took off to save both the woman and her hat, Triangle bounding at his heels.

He spent the next hour talking with his guests about animal habitats, what the various animals ate, and what they needed to feel safe and comfortable. Sometime in the middle of that hour, he relaxed. This was what he'd envisioned years ago. It was what he'd wanted to do for as long as he could remember, and a deep contentment flooded his heart.

When Seth signaled it was time for dinner, they walked next door to the Troyer home.

Grace's *dat* had placed three picnic tables out under the front fir trees. They were adorned with tablecloths and small mason jars filled with wildflowers. It looked as if Grace had come around to his way of thinking. Plainly, she'd gone all out to make their guests feel at home.

When she stepped outside, wearing a fresh white apron over a peach-colored dress, Adrian felt his pulse accelerate. How had he not noticed how pretty Grace was? Holding a basket of freshly baked bread and with Nicole clutching the hem of her dress, he couldn't think of anything that better personified their Amish life than the two of them.

He hurried over to her. "Anything I can do to help?"

"*Ya.* Carry these rolls over to the first table, then come back for the pitchers of water and tea."

For the next twenty minutes, he hurried between the tables and the kitchen. Grace's *mamm* sat at one table and her *dat* sat at the other. There was a place for him at the third. The *Englischers* soon felt comfortable enough to ask questions, and laughter could be heard as the chicken casserole was passed around the table.

Adrian was relaxed and happy and hopeful.

If all the tours went this well, word would get around. They'd soon be filled to capacity both Tuesday and Thursday evenings, and hopefully all involved would be willing to add a third weeknight tour or possibly a Saturday one.

The day had gone better than he could have hoped.

Then he took a bite of the casserole, nearly choked and realized that perhaps things weren't going so well after all.

He attempted to swallow the bite, found he couldn't and reached for his glass of water to wash it down. Had Grace dumped the entire box of salt in the casserole? He tried another bite and found it no better.

Adrian's temper rarely showed itself. He couldn't remember the last time something had caused his pulse to rocket, his muscles to quiver and a red tint to descend over his vision.

And yet all of those things were happening as he tried to understand how Grace could have done this.

What would possess her to stoop to sabotage?

And what was he going to do about it?

Chapter Three

"I'm sure I don't know what you're talking about." Grace snatched up a casserole dish that was still half full and strode into the house.

She hoped that would stop him. She hoped that maybe Adrian would go back to his menagerie next door and leave her alone. Why couldn't he concede defeat?

"You purposely made terrible food. How could you do such a thing?"

"Adrian, I have a lot of work to do cleaning these dishes. Perhaps we should talk about this later." Her *mamm* had taken Nicole upstairs for her bath, and her *dat* was checking on the two buggy horses. Unfortunately, that left her alone with Adrian.

"Later? As in, after you poison our next group of guests?"

"Salt is not poison."

"So that's what you did."

She mentally slapped her forehead. The idea was not to confess to Adrian, and honestly—anyone could accidentally add a little too much salt or pepper, or half a bottle of garlic powder.

"I don't understand, is all. How could you do such a thing?"

"Because I don't want *Englischers* traipsing all over our farm. I told you that." She turned on him suddenly, catching him by surprise. The look of confusion on his face tugged at her conscience, but it didn't weaken her resolve. She was doing this for Nicole. She was protecting her child. She needed to stand firm.

"Have you had any success looking for a new dinner stop?"

"I haven't had time to even begin checking into that, what with trying to get the place ready and then spending extra time with Cinnamon, who is not feeling safe in her new pen yet."

Grace did not want to talk about Adrian's camel. Honestly, she felt as if she'd stepped into a scene straight from a Doctor Doolittle movie—one of the few she'd seen as a rebellious teenager.

She stomped outside to grab another armful of dishes, Adrian dogging her heels.

At least he was able to carry quite a few plates at once. Why had they not opted for paper plates? *Englischers* were used to casual dining, but her *mamm* had insisted that anyone eating at her house would eat on a proper plate. She'd claimed it was important that each guest left fully satisfied, which succeeded in making Grace feel even more guilty. Her parents actually wanted the tours to be a success. She was surrounded by people who were determined to make this foolish scheme work.

The only trouble was they didn't realize what was at stake—her *doschder*'s safety.

As she plunged her hands into the dishwater, it occurred to her that perhaps Adrian wasn't her problem.

Her problem was that no one understood why she was so against this. Maybe she should talk to someone about her worries, about Nicole and about Nicole's father.

The few times she'd tried to broach the topic, her mother had created a lame excuse to leave the room. Once she'd even muttered *Best to leave the past behind you, dear.*

If only things were that simple.

"Where did you go?"

Grace jumped at the nearness of Adrian's voice, spraying them both with soapy dishwater.

"Sorry."

"It's okay." He accepted the dish towel she handed him and swiped at his shirt. "I know you said you don't want Nicole around strangers, and that you can't explain why, but I want to understand."

Instead of answering, Grace turned back to the tower of dirty dishes, tears stinging her eyes. Why was she so emotional? Because she wanted to talk to someone. She wanted a friend or confidant. She didn't need romance. That had been her mistake to begin with—thinking that Nicole's father could offer her a new and more meaningful life. Romance couldn't do that.

But a friend? A friend was something that she sorely needed. Maybe Adrian could…

What was she thinking?

She was a terrible judge of men.

She could handle this by herself.

So instead of answering Adrian, she took her frustrations out on the dishes, scrubbing them with renewed vigor. To her surprise, Adrian picked up a dish towel and began drying. They worked in silence, until the entire tower of dishes was washed, dried and put away.

When they were nearly done, he stepped next to her—close enough that their shoulders were touching—and said, "Can I have your word that you won't ever do that again? It's not fair to the guests who pay *gut* money for a decent meal."

Of course he was right, which only made her feel worse.

"*Ya*, you have my word."

She wasn't conceding, though. Fine, she'd cook delicious meals, but perhaps she could dissuade this dinner idea another way. She had a few ideas that had kept her tossing and turning the night before. Not that she planned to share those with Adrian. Instead, she smiled up at him, and said, "Or maybe I won't even need to cook again. Maybe you'll find someone else."

Which earned her a frown and a growl.

Ha ha. She was plainly annoying him. Excellent.

By that point, her *dat* had walked through the kitchen, declaring, "Guests wear me out. Think I'll put my feet up and read the *Budget*."

She rolled her eyes. Unfortunately, Adrian caught the expression and started laughing. Leaning closer and lowering his voice, he said, "It's not as if he spent all day cooking."

"What I was thinking exactly."

"Even if it was terrible cooking."

She gave him her most pointed look, tossed her *kapp* strings over her shoulders and began scrubbing the stove clean. Instead of leaving, Adrian took the dishrag, rinsed it, and began wiping down the table and counters.

"Don't you have animals to look after?"

"*Ya*. I do, but I know cooking can be a lot of work. At least that's what someone once told me."

Grace didn't know how to answer that, so she didn't. His kindness made her feel lousy about the deception. Fortunately, her *mamm* came into the kitchen at that moment.

"Adrian, I'm surprised you're still here."

"Oh, I wanted to help Grace with the cleanup phase."

"Well, I would certainly say today was a success, despite the problem with the casseroles. And Grace, that can happen to anyone. I once added Worcestershire to a dish that called for soy sauce." She pulled out the knitting she kept in a basket and sat at the table. "Yes, I would say that tonight was a real success. I sold quite a few of my knitted pieces, and the money will come in handy. Hopefully, word will spread. This was a *gut* idea, Adrian. Thank you for involving us."

A fresh stream of guilt washed over Grace.

As if reading her mind, her *mamm* added, "And I'm sure Grace will do a better job with the food next time. Probably just nerves."

Adrian rested his back against the counter, crossing his arms. "If you could have seen the old gent's face when he took a bite…"

Why was he always so comfortable in any situation? You'd think he'd been in their kitchen a dozen times, which Grace knew was not the case.

"The bread was *gut*, though. Everyone ate a lot of that, and most people had two helpings of dessert." Adrian looked at Grace and winked.

Good grief.

She was hoping he'd at least stay angry with her. She was counting on it. How else was she going to convince him to find a different cook?

"I better check on Nicole."

"She's sitting with your *dat* while he reads the paper. Why don't you walk Adrian outside?"

As if he couldn't find his way out. Grace didn't say that, though. Instead, she hung up the dish towel and motioned toward the front room.

She might have been okay with how the day had gone if it had ended there. Yes, she'd done a terrible thing, but no one was hurt and she'd done it for her child. Yes, she was exhausted, but hopefully she was putting this silly tour idea on the buggy lane to shutting down.

Overall, she felt optimistic.

Then they walked through the sitting room.

Nicole was sitting there, curled up next to her *daddi*, forefingers stuck in her mouth. When she saw Adrian, her entire face lit up. "Aden." She held up both hands and began to bounce.

"Look who's still up."

"Up."

Adrian scooped her into his arms. He held her high in the air, and when he brought her down, she snuggled in against his chest and put both arms around his neck, looking over his shoulder at Grace.

She felt as if a knife had ripped through the tissue of her heart. Her baby girl was safe and healthy. She should be grateful for that. Instead, she was reminded that Nicole needed a father—not to provide for her, Grace would do that. Her parents would do that. *Nein*, Nicole needed a father because every little girl should have the love of both parents.

And in that area, Grace had failed miserably.

Adrian didn't see Grace or Nicole at all the next day. He thought about them, though. He puzzled over Grace's desperate attempt to sabotage their *Englischer* tour. In some ways, he felt bad that he'd involved her. But in other ways, he thought it was a healthy thing. Her parents certainly considered the tour a *wunderbaar* idea, and the truth was that he thought Grace needed a little more contact with the outside world. She'd been home two months, and she rarely left the farm unless it was to attend church services.

Nein, he was doing the right thing.

The only issue was convincing Grace of that.

He spent Wednesday and Thursday sprucing up his place. The aviary needed a wider path through the middle so that guests could walk the entire length, and then there was the problem of his new camel. Cinnamon still wasn't feeling at home. He finally earned her trust with treats, then spent an hour brushing her. He'd never brushed a camel before, and he marveled at what an amazing creature she was.

Simon had given him a book on camels. It said the word *camel*, literally translated from the Arabic, meant *beauty*. When Adrian looked into Cinnamon's eyes, he could see why. He also quickly realized that he needed to keep an eye on the water level in her trough. The book claimed that a camel could drink forty gallons at once. He currently filled the animal's trough with a hand pump, so he'd have to monitor the water levels closely.

As he went about those tasks, his mind insisted on turning over the mystery of Grace. He'd never been one to tolerate an unsolved puzzle. As a teenager, he'd once spent an entire week putting together a jigsaw puzzle. His *dat* had bought it at a garage sale. The catch was that there was no box—no picture at all. Adrian had lived and breathed that puzzle for six-and-a-half days until he'd finally put the entire thing together. It had been a cat hanging on to a rope by its little paws, with the words Hang In There written underneath.

He needed to hang in there with Grace. Give her time to change her way of thinking.

Later that afternoon, Seth showed up at his farm with the tour group right on time, leading the line of buggies.

Adrian felt more comfortable with this second group. He didn't stumble over his words as he explained how he'd started the farm and why he provided a home for exotic animals. Kendrick didn't swipe anyone's hat, though he did spit on a gentleman. Fortunately, the man laughed and threatened to spit back. Cinnamon still wouldn't come near enough to be petted, but she did walk closer to the fence of her enclosure.

Overall, he felt that things were going very well.

When they walked over to Grace's place, he was surprised to see there were no picnic tables set up under the trees in front of the house. Grace was waiting for them on the front porch, once again looking as pretty as a picture from a story book. This time, Nicole was in her arms. As the guests gathered around the front porch, she said, "We thought that we'd have dinner tonight near the back of the property by the pond. My *dat* has hooked up the buggy horses to a trailer. You can either ride or walk."

Adrian sidled up close to her and lowered his voice. "A hayride is a *gut* idea. I should have thought of that."

"Well, you can't think of everything."

She gave him a winsome smile, and Adrian had the fleeting thought that something was up.

"Do I need to help you carry things?"

"*Nein*. It's all back there already. Fresh bread, sliced

ham, locally made cheese, potato salad and apple pie. There's no chance that I could ruin this meal."

Nicole reached for him, and Adrian pulled her into his arms. He hadn't realized how comforting it was to hold a child. He hadn't really considered himself father material, a worry that had only been reinforced by his lack of success in dating. He was more comfortable around animals than babies—except for Nicole. It felt natural to hold her, perhaps because she came to him so willingly. Adrian didn't know if he'd ever have a family of his own, but he wasn't giving up on the idea. He was still a young man, even though he had turned twenty-five.

Occasionally he realized that he'd like to court someone, that he'd enjoy caring for a family, but invariably he became distracted by his animals and his obligation to them. His animals, his dream of a sanctuary, had taken all of his time and attention. But holding Nicole, it occurred to him that perhaps he should try courting again. So what if previous attempts had been a disaster? Success came to the persistent.

He was so preoccupied with his thoughts, what Grace was saying to him hadn't quite registered. When she reached to take Nicole from him, he snapped out of his reverie.

"I can carry her."

"She's staying here at the house. Weren't you listening?"

His cheeks heated. "Oh. Guess my mind drifted a bit."

"She missed her nap today and has been a bit cranky."

Nicole waved her arm in the air, laughed, then stuck her fingers in her mouth.

"Do you need to stay with her?"

"*Nein.* Mamm will watch her. Then when the guests

come back to see her knitted things, I'll put Nicole to bed."

He nodded as if that made sense.

Grace was being awfully accommodating. Her attitude seemed completely different than two days ago. What had changed her mind? It hadn't been anything he'd said. Adrian was sure of that. She'd looked as petulant when he left on Tuesday evening as she had the day she had showed up at his place with a rolling pin. So what was going on?

She took Nicole inside, then returned with a shawl draped over her shoulders. It was a pretty lavender.

"That's a nice color on you."

"This? *Danki*. Mamm made it—of course." They started off toward the back of the property, walking at a brisk clip to catch up with the guests.

Adrian scratched his jawline, glanced in the direction they were going, then back at Grace. Why was she so happy? Why wasn't she asking him if he'd found another cook for the tour? This was too easy. In his experience, it took a longer amount of time for women to come around to someone else's way of thinking...which he immediately realized was a ridiculous thought. Men could be as stubborn as women.

Better to ask than to wonder. "Say, what's going on?"

"What do you mean?"

"Suddenly you seem on board with this."

"On board with what?"

"You know what I mean, with the tour group."

"Oh, that."

"Yes, that."

Grace increased her pace. How did someone with such small feet walk so fast?

"Tell me you haven't done anything to sabotage tonight's dinner."

"Of course not, Adrian." She smiled up at him sweetly, increasing his nervousness by several degrees. "On the other hand, I can't control everything."

What did that mean? Why was she still smiling? They'd reached the back of the property. She'd put a tablecloth on two old picnic tables and set out a few wellworn quilts by the small pond.

It was perfect. The entire thing was better than he could have imagined. So what was going on? Because for sure and certain, Grace Troyer was up to something.

The guests filled their plates and spread out to eat. His mind registered the fact that there were an awful lot of cut flowers in mason jars—and these weren't the wildflowers like they'd had on the tables on Tuesday. Stepping closer to the picnic table, he saw that they were actually tree blossoms.

They looked nice.

He filled his plate, and took a seat on one of the quilts. Small trays filled with tiny jars of peanut butter and jam were at each place, as well.

He didn't notice the bees at first, didn't understand immediately what was happening. First one guest, then another jumped up and began swatting at the air. By the time the bumblebees had fully invaded their picnic, hovering over the tree blossoms and investigating the peanut butter and jam, they had guests scattered everywhere. At first he couldn't spot Grace, but then he saw her sitting on the other side of the pond.

He couldn't believe it.

He could not accept that she would try to ruin their dinner again. Both hands on his hips, he scowled at her.

And what did Grace do? She shrugged her shoulders, hands held out, palms up. What had she said? *I can't control everything.*

Was he supposed to think this was a random, natural event?

He might not be able to prove it, but he knew the truth. And one way or another, he was going to get to the bottom of her issues. There was no way he was finding another place for his tour groups' dinners now. He'd set her straight about bumblebees and bad cooking and tour groups.

He accepted in that moment that Grace Troyer was not the same sweet young girl he'd gone to school with. She'd changed, and not for the better! Which was all good and fine with him.

He didn't need her to be his friend. He needed her to be his business partner, and he would find a way to make that happen.

After all, what else could she possibly do?

Chapter Four

Grace was out of ideas. She spent most of the weekend brooding over tour groups and *Englischers* and Adrian. Saturday, she scrubbed the house with such vigor that her *mamm* suggested she go easy on the floors or they'd have a hole in them soon. Sunday was a church day, but she couldn't focus on the singing or the sermons, and the new-members' class had only increased her angst. She felt like a fraud sitting among the other younger candidates. She'd already made so many mistakes in her life. How did one start over?

Their lesson had focused on the coming of Christ, something she'd heard about since she was a young girl and believed in with all her heart. She loved to think of heaven and being reunited with loved ones. But some days, heaven seemed a long ways off.

Grace sorely needed instruction on how to navigate the day-to-day of her life. She simply couldn't seem to get her feet underneath her. The service ended, but for Grace, the fellowship afterward was even worse.

All the women her age who also had young children had husbands. They sometimes attempted to draw Grace into their conversations, but she thought it was more out of pity than a real offer of friendship. The younger girls who didn't have husbands were either dragging out their *rumspringa* or actively on the hunt for a man. She certainly had nothing to add to those discussions.

So for the most part, she kept to herself, helping with both the serving and the cleanup of the meal, and she always found an excuse to leave as early as possible. A few times she caught sight of Adrian. Once he was looking directly at her and talking to his friend George Miller. He offered a small wave, but she pretended not to see. Soon after that, she and Nicole left for home.

Grace was still determined to stop the tours, but she couldn't think of a way to accomplish that. Finally on Monday, her *mamm* recommended that she visit her *schweschder*'s, suggesting that the afternoon away would help her mood, which had admittedly been terrible.

"What's wrong with you?" Georgia was nursing her three-month-old son, Jerome.

Grace missed that closeness with Nicole. Now that her little girl had moved on to drinking from a sippy cup, she realized she should have treasured those moments. Nicole was sitting on the kitchen floor, playing with her cousin Ben. They were very close to the same age.

Georgia prodded her with her foot. "Are you going to answer me?"

"What was the question?"

"Why the somber mood? Why the frowns and sighs? What's wrong with you?"

"I'd tell you if I knew."

She really couldn't blame it all on Adrian and his *Englisch* tours. The tour groups were just bearing the brunt of her bad mood, but underneath those feelings of frustration, she felt deeply unsettled. She had no desire to examine that, so instead, she focused on thwarting Adrian's plans. At least she was aware of her coping strategies. That had to count for something.

"Maybe it's the baby blues. You can have those, even after they're toddlers. I know, because after my oldest started walking I went through a bad patch of it."

"Maybe."

"I'll tell you a funny story to cheer you up." Georgia always had a humorous story to share. There'd been six girls in the house when they were growing up, and she was the comedian of the group. She was also the closest in age to Grace. They'd always been more like friends than *schweschdern*, though even Georgia didn't know who Nicole's father was.

When Grace had first told her she was pregnant—and Georgia was the first person she'd shared that information with—her *schweschder* had enfolded her in a hug and told her not to worry.

"Love will find a way," she'd whispered.

A month later, Grace had been bussed off to live with a Mennonite *aenti* in Ohio.

Georgia resettled her babe at the other breast, then leaned back to tell her story. "Will purchased a dozen goats a month ago. Remember that?"

"Oh, *ya*. You were both quite excited about it."

"We were, though I kept telling him that he needed to reinforce the fencing. You know what Dat always says, if water can get through a fence—"

"Then goats can get through it."

"Exactly. Will kept putting off the fence repairs. I don't know if he didn't want to spend the money on the fencing supplies or simply had other things he'd rather do."

"The goats got through the fence."

"Are you going to let me tell this? It's funnier if I just tell it."

"Fine…" In spite of herself, Grace was interested in the story. She'd heard that goats could be a lot of trouble, which was part of the reason she was so surprised that Adrian had recently acquired eight of the pygmy variety.

They're small, he'd explained. *No trouble at all.*

Georgia raised Jerome to her shoulder and proceeded to rub his back in soft circles. "Will put the goats in the back pasture and assured me they'd be fine. They would try to get out every time one of us went back to check on them or feed them, but Will declared he was smarter than a goat."

"Will is pretty smart. Remember the time he fixed that old windmill?"

"Focus. So I'm on the front porch talking to Bishop Luke when I hear this crying from inside—*mamm, mamm*. That's what it sounded like. Well, from the noise, you would have thought that I had a dozen children instead of four, and of course my girls were in school, so only two were home. Still, I kept hearing their voices—*mamm, mamm*."

Grace pressed her fingertips against her lips. She could see where this was going.

"Those cries were immediately followed by the sound of something crashing—several things crashing. The bishop, he's beginning to look concerned, and finally he says that perhaps I should check on whatever is happening. So I hurry inside, the bishop right behind me. And what do you think I see?"

"Goats."

"Goats." Georgia laughed right along with Grace. Her

schweschder had always been good-natured. "They were on the table."

"Uh-uh."

"*Ya.* They were on the floor, in the pantry, even under the sink. You wouldn't think a dozen goats could fit in here, but they did."

"Goat," Ben declared from his place on the floor, then banged a wooden spoon against a pot.

"That's not the funniest part. Ben was standing in the middle of the goats, tears streaming down his face. The biggest goat had taken his cookie."

"Goat." Ben rocked up onto all fours and crawled over to his mother, pulling up and resting his cheek against her lap.

"I'm telling you, it's amazing he wasn't traumatized, and praise *Gotte* I had the baby in my arms. Best I could tell, they'd busted through the screen of the back door. I'd left the actual door open because it was such a pretty day. But those goats scattered all over my kitchen, and Ben crying… It's a sight I'll remember even when Ben has children of his own."

Suddenly Grace felt better, because she had an idea how to stop the tours, one that might be seen as Adrian's fault instead of hers. After all, to the best of her knowledge, he had never reinforced his fence around the pasture where he was keeping the new pygmy goats. Also, it just happened to be located on the side of his property that shared a boundary with theirs. In fact, it was very near where they'd had the last picnic.

Which couldn't be a coincidence.

It felt…it felt more like providence.

The next morning, she rose in a better mood. It was true that a tour group—another *full* tour group of twenty people, Adrian had announced gleefully—was coming, but she had a plan that just might work this time.

When Nicole went down for her morning nap, Grace picked up the bowl of vegetable scraps and headed toward the fence line, toward Adrian's pygmy goats.

Thanks to Adrian's enthusiasm and her parents' willingness to listen to anything, she now knew all about pygmy goats.

They grew as tall as fifteen to twenty inches.

Does could weigh thirty-five to fifty pounds. Males usually weighed in at forty to sixty.

Basically, they were the size of a medium dog.

She was prepared not to like them, but there was something about goats that made a person laugh. She squatted at the fence line, feeding them carrot tops, wilted lettuce leaves and cucumber peels. She couldn't stop herself from reaching through the fence and touching their soft fur. Three were gray—ranging from a soft color, like a skein of yarn her mother knitted with, to a dark gray, like storm clouds. Two more were black with white splotches. And the final three reminded her of a box of chocolates her father had bought for Christmas one year—everything from light to medium to dark caramel.

Suddenly she found herself thinking of Adrian's eyes.

Adrian's eyes!

She stood, brushed her hands and checked the gate, which allowed access for her *dat* and Adrian to move more easily between the two properties. Apparently they were now working together on a few projects. The gate wasn't locked, only latched… It would be easy enough to slip it open after the guests arrived.

And really, a goat could do that without her help, if it had the right motivation.

She had more salad scraps in the kitchen.

It was as she was walking back toward the house that she came across her *dat* mending a harness for the workhorses. He smelled of dirt and crops and horses. He smelled like the father who had been there for her all her life. Though he was a man of few words, she understood that he loved her and Nicole, and that he would always provide for them.

"Hold this for me while I mend the strap?"

"Sure."

They worked without talking, a comfortable, peaceful silence, until he'd finished and thanked her. She'd begun to walk away when he called out to her.

"Adrian's a *gut* man."

She turned, cocked her head and waited.

"I know you don't agree with this tour thing. I know it's hard for you."

"That's true, and I have good reasons—"

"I don't need to know why, Grace. The fact that it is hard for you, that's what matters. I'm sorry for that. But this farm needs all the income it can earn... Our family needs all the income we can earn. We won't be passing up *gut* work that the Lord provides for us. That would be wrong, in my opinion." Then he turned back to the harness, having said his piece.

Leaving Grace wondering if she really wanted to follow through with her plan to put a stop to Adrian's tour groups once and for all.

The third tour group could not have gone better. Adrian was growing quite comfortable with talking in front of groups, and the tourists seemed generally interested in his animals. His favorite part, though, was when they wandered off on their own and enjoyed God's creations. That was when he noticed the smiles blooming and the worry lines draining away, as if for a moment at least, they had laid down a burden.

He arrived at Grace's place, surprised to find her *mamm* greeting the group and directing them toward the back pond.

Seth led the group that wanted to walk, while Grace's *dat* helped the others onto the hayride. Adrian held back.

"Something wrong, Adrian?" Grace's *mamm* had always been kind yet to the point. No use trying to beat around the bush with Leslie Troyer.

"I didn't see Grace, and I was wondering if she's *oll recht.*"

"Grace is already at the back pasture with Nicole. She wanted to make sure everything was perfect when the *Englischers* arrived."

"Or sabotage it," he muttered under his breath, but Leslie heard him.

If she was offended, she didn't show it. Instead, she walked down the porch steps carrying a large basket of hot rolls. He could smell the yeast and butter, and it caused his stomach to growl.

"Let's walk together."

"I didn't mean to be rude."

"You were only being honest. We both know that the ruined casseroles and bumblebees weren't a mistake."

"If you knew, why didn't you—"

"Stop her?" Leslie shrugged. "First off, I didn't know until after the fact. And secondly, have you ever tried to stop Grace when she has her mind set on something?"

"Then the tours are doomed."

"Maybe not."

"I don't understand why she's so dead set against them. In fact, I'd thought she would welcome a chance to make a little extra income."

"Her *dat* and I certainly do."

"But Grace…"

Leslie stopped, her attention on a week-old calf and the cow that was attending to it. She looked back at him, smiled and continued walking. He hurried to catch up with her. The Troyer women, they were all fast walkers.

"Was I supposed to understand something about Grace, based on that calf?"

"Oh, Adrian." Leslie's smile was genuine, and he couldn't have felt offended if he'd tried. She wasn't laughing at him, he was sure of that, but she was amused at the current situation.

"Grace has five *schweschdern*. Did you know that?"

"I suppose I've never stopped to count."

"And Grace is the youngest and closest to your age… No, maybe Georgia is the closest to your age."

"*Ya.* Georgia and I were in the same grade at school."

"So, six girls. We've been through quite a bit, as far as beaus and husbands and *bopplin*."

"I don't understand."

"My girls all have different personalities, though they are all stubborn to the core. They get that from their *dat*." She smiled at her joke.

They were in sight of the group now, and Leslie stopped, surveyed it, then turned to search his eyes.

"One thing I can tell you for certain is that each of those girls will do anything to protect and care for their children. Just like that cow and calf. It's nature's way. It's *Gotte*'s way."

"Okay, but how does a tour group threaten Nicole?"

"I don't know." She said it simply, and one thing that

Adrian understood in that moment was that she wasn't concerned at all. "*Gotte* will take care of Nicole. We can trust He will take care of all of us, but Grace is new at raising a child."

"It's so kind of Grace to raise her cousin's *bop-pli*." When Leslie gave him an odd look and waited, he crossed and uncrossed his arms. "I… What I mean to say is that I've tried, but it's hard to imagine taking on that kind of responsibility. I mean, I have responsibilities with the animals, but it's not the same."

Leslie glanced toward Grace, then back at Adrian.

He squirmed under her gaze, but he waited. He felt like there was something he needed to understand about this conversation. But he didn't.

"For whatever reason, Grace is being extra careful with Nicole. The thing is… The reason doesn't matter."

"It doesn't?"

"Adrian, I think you've hitched the buggy in front of the horse."

"What?"

She patted his arm. "Stop trying to figure out what Grace is concerned about and just get to know her."

She walked off toward the group that was now once again scattered around the pond and at the picnic tables. Grace was walking from group to group, a pitcher of tea in one hand, holding Nicole on her hip with the other.

Just get to know her.

He had been thinking of Grace as a means to an end. He resisted the urge to slap his forehead with his hand. Basically, he was using her. No wonder she didn't trust him. And the worry about *Englischers* around Nicole? He didn't have to understand that. After all, she was Nicole's *mamm*. She knew what was best for her child.

How arrogant of him to think that he might know more on that topic than she did.

Grace looked up at that moment, and Adrian smiled and waved—as he had done at church. This time instead of ignoring him, she smiled back and nodded, then turned her attention to the *Englischer* who was asking for more tea.

The meal progressed well. The food was delicious. No bees attacked. It was… It was picture-perfect. Adrian began to relax and enjoy himself. He began to wonder about how he might get to know Grace Troyer.

In fact, where was she?

He checked each group but didn't see her. Leslie was watching over Nicole, who was yawning and sticking her two fingers into her mouth. Adrian turned in a circle, looking for Grace, and saw her standing next to the fence line, right before his goats crashed through the gate and made a beeline for the picnic.

Immediately there were pygmy goats everywhere— in the pond, on the tables, and one was even tugging on an *Englisch* woman's purse. His smallest goat had taken an interest in a tablecloth and was trying to pull it off the table. An *Englisch* man grabbed the other end and proceeded to engage in a bizarre tug-of-war.

Nicole was pointing and laughing.

James and Seth were attempting to herd the goats back toward the fence.

Leslie had grabbed the platter with the coconut cake and was holding it above her head as two of the goats bumped against her legs.

And Grace…

Grace was standing at the fence line, a huge smile on her face.

Chapter Five

It took a half hour to gather up the goats and move them back to their side of the fence. Grace was dismayed to note that the *Englischers* seemed more entertained than perturbed. Several had pulled out their phones and snapped pictures. She even heard one woman say, "I'd heard about these tours. Someone posted on their blog that you could always count on a surprise twist. Wait until I tell my daughters about these goats. What a hoot!"

Her plan had clearly backfired.

Grace expected Adrian to confront her, but although he looked in her direction several times, he didn't seek her out. She was a little disappointed, as she had her defense all ready.

First, he needed a better latch on the gate.

Second, she'd agreed not to sabotage the dinner and she hadn't. The cooking was spot-on.

And third, well, she didn't have a third reason, but she would have come up with one if he'd asked.

He didn't.

He left with Seth after the *Englischers* had tramped through their house and bought more of her *mamm*'s knitting—receiving blankets and baby booties and small sweaters with matching hats.

"Good thing I have a large amount of items completed already." Her *mamm* glanced up and smiled, then waved the money she was about to put into the mason jar they kept for emergencies. Most of their income went in the bank, what little they had. But the mason jar was the extra-money jar. It paid for birthday gifts and doctors' visits and dinners out. "Two hundred and forty dollars, Grace. It's a real blessing for sure."

How could Grace argue with that?

Adrian didn't stop by that evening or the next morning, but toward dinner on Wednesday, he knocked on the front door. Did she imagine it, or did he purposely show up when they were about to eat? Not that she could blame him. No doubt his cooking skills were limited, and his kitchen—well, it could hardly be called that.

Grace had made a casserole that combined ground beef, cheese and noodles. She served it with a side salad and green beans, and for dessert, she'd made oatmeal pie. As aggravated as she was with him, something in Grace wanted to feed Adrian. Maybe it was her nesting instincts. Maybe it was the fact that he was so tall and thin. If he turned sideways you could look his direction and miss him. Okay, he wasn't that thin, but nearly.

Whatever the reason, she waved him to the seat across from her and hopped up to fetch an extra plate.

Dinner conversation jumped back and forth between the topics of crops, animals and church. No one mentioned tour groups, although it seemed to Grace that they must be on everyone's mind. It was almost as if they were afraid of setting her off.

She wasn't an ogre.

She didn't lash out at people.

Though she had to admit her behavior had been less than stellar. In fact, she wasn't proud of the steps she'd taken to put a stop to the tours. They had seemed necessary at the time. Had they truly been necessary? Had she been wrong? She'd been quite conflicted about her sabotage efforts the evening before as she'd read her Bible. She'd been working her way through the gospels, and the twelfth chapter of Mark seemed to be written specifically to her.

Love thy neighbor as thyself.

That was the problem with the Bible. It was so black-and-white. It didn't leave much room for her justifying her actions. Still, she could defend what she'd done. She was protecting her child. What if Nicole's father showed up, out of the blue, and demanded joint custody? What would she do then?

Nein. She couldn't conceive such a thing.

So what if she added too much salt to a dinner or attracted bees or unleashed goats? No one was hurt by her actions. Perhaps Adrian would grow tired of her antics and find another cook.

The *Englischers* would stop coming by the farm, and Nicole would be safe.

Love thy neighbor as thyself.

She certainly wouldn't want to be served a bad-tasting meal, and some people were afraid of bees. As far as the goats, everyone had been entertained by the little pygmies, which was beside the point. In truth, she was rather ashamed of herself but didn't know what to do about it.

When she began clearing the dishes, Adrian once again dried and put things away as she washed.

"You don't have to do that."

"Help?"

"Yes, help."

"You don't want help?"

"I don't understand why you're standing here in my kitchen holding a dish towel." Her face, neck and ears suddenly felt unbearably hot. She wondered if she was coming down with something. "I don't understand the *why* of it."

"Why what?"

"Why do you want to help me, Adrian? Don't you need to get back to your zoo?"

"Even I grow tired of animals now and then. Their conversation isn't as *gut* as yours."

Which was patently not true. She was a terrible conversationalist. She never knew what to say to a man. They'd already covered the safe topics at dinner. Would Adrian be interested in hearing about Nicole's latest achievements? The way she'd smiled up at Grace when she fetched her from her nap or that she'd patted Grace's face and said "mine"? Had she meant "*mamm*"? Or had she claimed Grace as her own? Why would Adrian want to hear about any of that?

Maybe she was overthinking everything.

She wasn't sure.

Having grown tired of waiting for a response, Adrian nudged her shoulder with his. "I saw that Nicole was standing in the middle of the room earlier—without holding on to a thing."

"Did you see that?" Grace beamed with pleasure, as if she had something to do with Nicole's standing ability. "She's a smart girl."

"Indeed."

"Earlier today, she squatted to pick up a toy."

"Squatted?"

"*Ya.* It's an important milestone, or so my *Milestones for Your Child* book states."

"There's a book called *Milestones for Your Child*?"

"Not my point. Up until then, if she wanted something, she would crawl over, plop down and then drag it toward herself."

"But today she squatted?"

"She did." Grace laughed with him. "Sounds like a small achievement, I know, but it filled my heart with joy. She was holding on to the coffee table, walking around it and laughing, as she does when she thinks she's getting away from something."

"She's a *gut*-natured child."

"And then she saw her baby doll on the floor. She pivoted, squatted and picked up the doll." Grace plunged her hands back into the soapy water. "Children are amazing."

"Indeed they are. Reminds me of Cinnamon."

"My child reminds you of your camel?"

"Hear me out." Adrian brought her up-to-date on how nervous the camel had been when it had first arrived at his farm and the progress they'd made since then. "I believe she was afraid of people, though I have no idea why she would be. Perhaps the man I purchased her from only interacted with her to feed her or milk her. Did I tell you about the milking?"

"*Ya.* I still can't believe it sold for so much. I've never even heard of people drinking camel milk."

"Anyway, at first she'd stand across the pen and stare at me suspiciously. Now, if I'm alone, she trots right over to me."

"How does she get along with the other animals?"

"I believe she's taken a liking to Triangle, my dog."

"I know who Triangle is. That's an odd-looking mutt, but I'll admit he grows on a person."

"She doesn't seem to like Kendrick, though."

"Your llama has bad manners."

"Does not."

"Does Kendrick spit at her?"

"Now that you mention it…"

They again shared a smile, and Grace was suddenly glad that Adrian had stopped by. It was nice to talk to someone other than her parents, and Nicole… She wasn't able to hold up her end of a conversation yet.

Grace had never been good at talking to men. Perhaps that came from being raised with only sisters. She wasn't sure. She did realize now that she'd been very shy as a teen, and she'd dated only in groups. Perhaps that was why she'd fallen for Nicole's father so quickly. He'd paid attention to her in a way that she'd never experienced.

That had immediately been followed by her year in exile.

And now she was home. She was older and more confident in some ways, and she suddenly found that talking to a boy—to a man—didn't seem nearly as intimidating as it once had.

Not that she expected anything to come of it, and maybe that was a plus. Maybe by taking the word *relationship* out of the equation, she was able to relax. She would like to be able to count Adrian as a friend.

Not that it would last. Adrian would eventually marry, and his *fraa* wouldn't want him gallivanting next door to wash dishes with the neighbor. But she was tired of worrying about the future. Perhaps, for just a little while, she could learn to appreciate the moment for what it was.

* * *

Adrian hated to ruin the nice conversation he was having with Grace. He could practically feel her relax, and she'd actually smiled a few times. It occurred to him that her life must be lonely here with her parents.

Why didn't she get out more?

Why didn't she date?

He nearly groaned in frustration. He was doing it again—trying to figure out how to fix her life.

Just get to know her.

One thing he understood for certain was how much she cared about Nicole, and that was the reason he'd come to talk to her.

"Would you like to take a walk?"

She looked at him as if he'd sprouted wings. "A walk?"

"It's a nice evening, warmer than it has been." He peered past her, out the window. "*Gut* sunset. Thought we might take Nicole to see some flowers I spied near your front lane."

She continued to look at him questioningly but stammered through a response that seemed more *yes* than *no* and ended with, "Let me fetch our sweaters."

At first they walked slowly down the lane, Nicole toddling between them, each holding one of her hands.

"She's not very fast yet. At this rate, we'll reach the fence line by sunrise." Grace attempted to pick up Nicole, who was having none of it.

She squirmed in her mother's arms, arched her back and said repeatedly, "No, no, no, no." Then she changed her chorus to, "Aden, Aden."

When Adrian reached for her, Grace's eyebrows arched in surprise, but she happily handed her over. "Fair warning—she grows heavier with each step you take."

Adrian was once again struck by how adorable and precious Nicole was. He thought maybe she was small for her age, but what she lacked in weight and height she made up for in attitude. Though she'd plopped her two fingers into her mouth, she pulled them out to shout unintelligible words at various things.

"Any idea what she's saying?"

"Not really."

When they reached the wooden fence that bordered the front lane, he led them to where he'd seen wildflowers— blue violets, Virginia bluebells, and a small white flower his mother called "spring beauties."

"Is it okay to let her down?"

"Sure, *ya*. Maybe she'll wear herself out."

Nicole glanced up at them, then toddled sideways, holding on to the bottom slat of the fence. When she squatted to pick one of the flowers, Adrian and Grace shared a smile.

"She's a pro at that now."

"Indeed."

"Emerson said that 'the earth laughs in flowers.'"

"What does that mean?"

"I don't know, but it comes to mind when I see so many." Adrian stuck his hands in his pockets, but his arms felt unnatural and awkward. He pulled them back out, then crossed them. Good grief. What was he so nervous about? "Say, Grace. I wanted to talk to you about Nicole."

Which was probably the wrong way to begin the conversation, since Grace instantly froze, the expression on her face one of caution and worry.

"It's nothing bad. It's just that I was thinking about

what you said—about not wanting Nicole around *Englischers*."

Still she only looked at him, and he knew then that she was expecting him to argue with her, to tell her how silly she was, to point out the importance of the tours.

He didn't do any of those things.

"My youngest *schweschder*, Lydia, she loves babies. She takes care of her nieces and nephews all the time. I was thinking that I could bring her over on tour nights, and she could stay with Nicole in the house, so she wouldn't have to be out with all the *Englischers*. I'd be happy to pay her out of my portion of the profits."

"Your *schweschder*?"

"Sure. You remember Lydia. Only I guess—" he glanced up at the trees, doing the math "—if she's fourteen, which I'm sure she is, and you're…"

"Twenty-three."

"So you're nine years older, which means you were out of school when she started."

"I know Lydia, Adrian. We all attend the same church meetings."

"Right. Of course."

"And that's a very kind suggestion." She took a crushed flower that Nicole pushed into her hand. "But why…? Why would you offer to do such a thing?"

"Because you're concerned about Nicole, and I want to ease your mind. If I can."

Grace studied her *doschder*, then turned and looked at Adrian.

"It would help, probably more than you can imagine. I would definitely worry about her less if she was, you know, playing inside."

"Exactly, and Lydia is happy to do it."

"You've asked her already?"

"I suggested that I might know someone who needed her help a couple hours a week. I didn't make any commitment on your part. I wouldn't do that without checking with you first."

Nicole became suddenly mesmerized by a butterfly. She reached a chubby finger out to touch it, laughed when it fluttered up and then back down again. Looking at Grace, she said, "Bird."

"Butterfly." Grace picked her up and kissed her neck, inhaling deeply.

Nicole stared over Grace's shoulder at Adrian, stuck the requisite two fingers in her mouth and watched him solemnly. When Grace turned back toward him, he knew that he'd finally said and done the right thing.

"That was very thoughtful of you, Adrian. *Danki.*"

"Gem gschehne."

"We accept."

"Wunderbaar."

"On one condition."

"Uh-oh."

"I will pay Lydia from *my* earnings." When Adrian tried to protest, she held up a hand like a traffic cop. "It's only fair, since she'll be watching my *doschder.*"

He loved that about Grace. She treated Nicole as her own. He might never know the details of Nicole's birth, but he did know with certainty that the little girl in front of him would never lack for love or family. Grace would see to both of those things.

"All right, but my intent wasn't to lessen what you earn."

"I know that. You want your tours to be a success."

"Yup."

"Which means no more cooking mishaps."

"Your last meal was delicious." For some reason, he was no longer angry when he thought of that first meal, maybe because that particular fiasco hadn't been repeated.

"No more bees," Grace added.

"Bees don't really scare me."

"And no more goats."

"I have to admit, it was rather funny when Nelly tried to snatch the woman's purse."

"You've named your goats?"

"Well, *ya*. Every animal appreciates…being appreciated." He was suddenly aware of the way the last of the day's light played across Grace's hair. Of course most of it was covered with her *kapp*, but a good bit of the part at the front had escaped.

Why was he surprised that her hair was somewhat curly?

He looked at Nicole, then back at Grace. The two looked very much alike… That must be a coincidence. Well, probably Grace's cousin looked like Grace, so it would make sense that her cousin's baby girl would look like Grace.

He wondered again about that situation. Why had Grace agreed to raise Nicole? Would her natural *mamm* want her back at some point?

"You're too good-natured, Adrian."

"Can a person be too good-natured?"

They were walking back toward the house, the sky afire with orange, purple and blue clouds as the sun set upon what Adrian thought had been a very good day. Which had nothing to do with the woman and child walking beside him. It was more that the conflict in his life had suddenly dissipated. Adrian wasn't a fan of conflict. That might be why he sought the company of animals and occasionally avoided people.

Animals were predictable—except for the goats and possibly Cinnamon. Kendrick could be a challenge at times. Mostly, though, he understood why his animals did what they did. Cinnamon hadn't been properly socialized. Kendrick was a little bored. Animals were fairly easy creatures to figure out.

People, on the other hand, were much harder to read. He often didn't understand why they acted the way that they did. But Grace? Grace he could understand. Regardless the reason for her raising Nicole, there was no doubt that she dearly loved the child.

They'd nearly reached the porch steps when he thought to thank her for dinner.

"You don't have to thank me, Adrian. I would have cooked anyway."

"Still, it was nice of you to share." He shifted a sleepy Nicole to his other arm. "I love my farm, and living in the barn isn't a problem, but you know what I really miss?"

Grace shook her head, then ran her fingers up and down her *kapp* strings and waited, almost as if she were interested. He took that as a positive sign and pushed on.

"Ice cream."

"Ice cream?"

"*Ya.* I have a small refrigerator but no freezer." He rubbed a hand over his jaw. "A pint of Ben & Jerry's would hit the spot."

"Ben and Jerry's? You go for the good stuff, then."

"I do. Salted Caramel Almond is my absolute favorite." He slipped Nicole into her arms, and for a moment, they were standing closer than they ever had, close enough that he could smell shampoo and soap and the freshness of the spring evening that seemed to have settled on Grace. She glanced up at him, a smile playing on her lips.

"That's a real tragedy, Adrian."

"It is."

"Maybe you should build a house someday."

"Or at least purchase a proper refrigerator."

Her laughter did more to lift his spirits than a dozen pints of ice cream. As he walked back to his place, it occurred to him that caring for God's animals was all good and fine, but people needed the companionship of other people.

The question was whether he was willing to do anything about it.

His mood sank at that thought. Every woman he'd tried to date had quickly pointed out that he spent too much time and money on animals, that he didn't live in a proper house, that he had his priorities wrong. Women didn't understand him. If he ever found someone who did, he would probably have to compromise, make some changes to his life.

Was he willing to do that?

Things were finally going well.

Which was why it would be ridiculous to entertain the idea of courting anyone now. Maybe in a few years. Maybe when he'd built a proper house, with a proper refrigerator, with a freezer that could hold several pints of Ben & Jerry's ice cream.

Chapter Six

The next day's tour went perfectly. Grace actually enjoyed cooking the meal, the tourists were pleasant, and her *mamm* once again sold quite a few items—including some market bags and prayer shawls she'd quickly knitted up. She also sold a couple of lap quilts that Grace's oldest *schweschder* had sent over. Greta was a very talented quilter, something Grace had never mastered. Oh, she could attend a frolic and do her part, but she didn't put fabrics together the way that Greta did. Her *schweschder* had a real gift.

But more than all those things, Grace was happy about having Lydia to look after Nicole. Lydia was sitting on the floor playing with her *doschder* when Grace left to oversee the dinner, and she was rocking her in a chair in the bedroom when she returned. The two seemed to have bonded instantly.

Lydia was thin, nearly as tall as Grace and wore glasses with blue frames. The fact that she carried a book in the pocket of her apron made Grace laugh.

"There's always time to read when you're waiting on someone," Lydia explained.

Grace couldn't have asked for the evening to have gone better. She still wasn't convinced that *Englisch* tours were something they should be doing. It continued to feel odd turning their home into a commercial venture, but since her parents had already made up their minds, she might as well get on board.

Then the next morning, Nicole woke in a fussy mood.

"Maybe she's teething again," her *mamm* suggested.

But she wasn't teething. That was always accompanied by excessive drooling. Grace had even sewn up some bibs to put on her during those times. This was different. Nicole whimpered, didn't want any of her toys, wouldn't even look at her *daddi*, who always made her smile, and insisted on Grace sitting down to hold her.

"You know what they say." Her *mamm* was knitting a new baby blanket at breakneck speed. She'd just cast it on that morning, and she had already progressed a good twelve inches. The colors were a soft, variegated baby blue, yellow and pink.

"I'm afraid I don't."

"Cleaning, quilting, cooking… Those things will wait."

"They will?"

"But the years when you can hold your child in your lap, those will pass in the blink of an eye."

By midafternoon, Nicole's cheeks were two red spots and she was tugging at her ear.

"Best take her in to the doctor," her *mamm* suggested.

"Do you think it's that serious?"

"Fevers usually rise at night, and the poor thing seems so miserable." Her *mamm* stored her knitting needles, pressed a hand to Nicole's cheek, then kissed her softly on the top of her head. "I'll go and ask your *dat* to ready the buggy."

Her *mamm* drove and Grace held Nicole in her arms. The day was overcast with a slight drizzle, and the temps had turned cooler once again. Grace had rather enjoyed the week of warm, sunny days. Now the skies seemed to reflect her feelings—worry pressing down on her heart as the clouds pressed down over the fields. She knew the weather and her mood wouldn't last, but for the moment, she was practically overwhelmed by concern and sadness and fear.

"Do you think it's serious?"

"It could be many things, Grace. Doc Amanda will know what to do."

Doc Amanda had been Grace's doctor. She'd set up practice in the Goshen community before Grace was born, which meant the woman had to be getting up in age. Grace hadn't had a need to see her since returning home, though she had called and made Nicole's fifteen-month appointment for the following month. The pediatrician in Ohio had been a young man whose office was a bit austere. Although he seemed like a good doctor, and Grace had faithfully taken Nicole for her checkups, she'd never felt completely comfortable there.

So she walked into Doctor Amanda's office with some hesitancy. It didn't last long. There were low tables with toys for children, new magazines for harried parents, even a coffee center set up behind a counter with a sign that read Help Yourself.

They had been waiting only a half hour when the nurse called Nicole's name. As Grace juggled her purse, diaper bag and child, her *mamm* stood and pushed a wad of bills into her hands. "From the mason jar."

"But *Mamm*…"

"That's what the emergency money is for, Grace. Now go."

She expected to wait a long time in the small examining room. The walls were decorated with growth charts and animal pictures, which immediately reminded her of Adrian. But Nicole wasn't interested in measuring her height or looking at animals. She sat curled up on Grace's lap, her fingers in her mouth, an occasional whimper escaping her lips.

The nurse popped into the room with a bright smile. She wore scrubs covered with rainbows and unicorns, and her hair was pulled back into a high ponytail. She asked the standard questions, entered the information into a tablet, then took Nicole's temperature, which was a disturbingly high 102.

Ten minutes later, Doc Amanda tapped on the door. She walked in, placed the tablet on the counter and walked over to a sink to wash her hands. Once she'd dried them, she pulled a chair up in front of Grace so that they were sitting knee to knee.

"It's good to see you, Grace. It's been a while."

"A long while."

"And this must be Nicole."

"We have her fifteen-month appointment in a few weeks for her vaccinations."

"I'm glad to hear you're keeping up with those."

"When she started running a fever, I thought I should bring her in today. She's…she's not well."

"You did the right thing." Doc Amanda turned her attention to Nicole. "Hey, baby girl. Want to play with my stethoscope?"

Nicole buried her face in Grace's dress, and Doc

Amanda was easily able to pop the tip of her instrument into Nicole's ear.

"Definitely an ear infection."

"*Ya?* But you can give her something?"

"I can, and I will. Let's check the other side first."

Which was a little trickier. Nicole didn't want to turn her head and immediately began crying and murmuring, "No, Mamm. No."

"Two-word sentences. Very good."

Doc Amanda finally managed to take a peek in the other ear, then listened to her breathing and looked into her eyes.

"The left ear has an infection. The right one looks a bit irritated, so she could be getting an infection there, as well. Don't be surprised if you see her pulling on both. A little medicine should fix Nicole right up. Let's try the pink stuff."

"Pink stuff?"

"Amoxicillin. My kids call it the pink stuff." She tapped something into the tablet. "What pharmacy do you use?"

"I haven't needed one."

Doc Amanda looked up from the tablet. "You moved away for a while."

Grace wasn't exactly surprised that she knew. Doc Amanda was the pediatrician most Amish families in the area used, and little went unnoticed in a small town. But Grace realized there was an opportunity here, and honestly, she was ready to be truthful with someone.

"Yes. I moved to Ohio while I was pregnant with Nicole. My family thought it was best if I stayed with an *aenti*."

"Well, it's good to have you back."

"Danki."

"And it's good to meet Nicole. She's a beautiful child. She looks a lot like you."

Why did those words send a surge of joy through Grace's heart? It was silly, really. Of course a child would look like her mother, though Grace had often wondered if Nicole looked more like her or her father. It was difficult to tell when you were so close to someone, and there was no one she could ask, since no one knew that Nicole was hers.

She was suddenly glad that she'd been honest with Doctor Amanda. It helped that someone knew her situation and didn't judge her.

The doctor was still tapping on the tablet. "Goshen has grown a bit in the last few years."

"It certainly has."

"We have several pharmacies—the biggest is at the Walmart."

"That's on the opposite side of town from where we live."

"How about Meijers grocery store?"

"Yes, that would be better. I could pick up some other items while I'm there."

Doctor Amanda stood and plucked a handout from the counter where she'd washed her hands. "Here's a sheet on reducing fever in toddlers. You'll want to pick up something for that, as well. She should be feeling better in twenty-four to forty-eight hours. If not, come back and see me again, or you could call and we'll prescribe a stronger antibiotic. I like to start with the pink stuff, and it usually works."

"Danki."

"You're very welcome, and I look forward to spend-

ing a little more time with Nicole when she comes in for
her regular checkup."

Nicole was still burning with fever and pulling on
her ear, but now they had a plan. That made Grace feel
immeasurably better. As she paid with the wad of bills
her mother had pressed into her hand, it wasn't lost on
her that they had extra money largely due to Adrian. Because of the tours, she didn't have to worry how much
the medicine cost or whether she should buy one bag of
diapers or two at the store.

Many people thought that all Amish babies wore only
cloth diapers, and certainly she did use cloth when it
made sense to do so. But when they were at church or
out in public, she popped on a disposable. Her *mamm*
waited on a bench at the front of the supermarket with
Nicole as Grace gathered up supplies, including a few
things they needed in the grocery section.

She was on her way to the checkout line when she
passed the ice cream freezers.

Ice cream.

What was it Adrian had said he liked?

She backtracked and hunted around until she came
away with a pint of Salted Caramel Almond. Then she
added a vanilla to share with her *mamm* and Nicole, and
Chunky Monkey for her *dat*. Three pints of ice cream
was a splurge, but suddenly she felt like celebrating.

After all, she had the money for it in her pocket.

She had the medicine for her daughter in her purse.

And she had Adrian's tours to thank for both.

It was Monday morning when Adrian learned that Nicole was sick. He was helping Grace's *dat* mow the area
around the back pond, which was where their guests ap-

parently enjoyed dinner the most. The recent light rains they'd had seemed to have caused the grass to grow a foot. Everything was green and spring-like, and Adrian was thinking of how much he was looking forward to their next tour group, when James pulled him out of his daydreams.

"Leslie might be cooking tomorrow's meal."

"Why's that?"

"Baby girl has been sick—she had an ear infection."

"Is she okay? Does Grace need anything? Does Nicole need—?"

James held up his hand to stop the flood of questions. "The first medicine didn't work, so Doc Amanda called out something stronger. It's been a tough few days for both Grace and Nicole, for all of us, really. When the baby doesn't sleep, no one sleeps."

"I had no idea." In that moment, Adrian realized it wasn't the tour group he'd been looking forward to as much as it was seeing Grace again.

He'd spent quite a bit of time thinking about their walk to the fence line. He'd reached the conclusion that he'd like to be friends—close friends—with Grace. Nothing romantic, of course. He knew zilch about courting a woman, and he wasn't really in the right place to do so from a financial standpoint. But friendship? That he was ready for.

"Is there anything I can do?"

"Nicole was better this morning, but poor Grace. After three nights of very little sleep, she's a bit of a mess."

"I guess so."

"She's finding out what it means to be a *mamm*—fortunately, the good outweighs the bad, which is one reason we all have so many children."

"I guess. I mean, I'm sure Nicole is a great kid. It's just that I don't have any experience in that area."

"You have nieces and nephews."

"True, though I suspect that's drastically different from having your own."

"What are you waiting for?"

Adrian looked up from the mowed grass that he was raking out of the picnic area. For a moment, he was confused by the question, then he realized that James was asking him why he wasn't married, why he hadn't started a family. "I'm not sure what I'm waiting for. The right time? The right person?"

James laughed. "In my experience, the right time is now."

"I don't know…"

"As for the right person, that's often someone you already know, but simply have to look at in a different light."

Wait a minute… Was he dropping a hint?

Did Grace's *dat* want him to court her?

Before he could think of how to ask either of those questions, James had started up the diesel-powered weed eater again and was proceeding around the pond.

Adrian spent the rest of the time he was doing yard work with his thoughts bouncing around in his head. On the one hand, he was consumed with concern for Grace and Nicole. On the other hand, he was puzzled. Why had James brought up families and marriage? Both were distracting thoughts, which he couldn't shake even after he went back to his place. He found himself dumping bird food in Kendrick's feed bucket and trying to groom Cinnamon with a dog brush.

You could have knocked him over with a feather

duster when Grace showed up at his place an hour before sunset.

"Is Nicole okay?"

"*Ya.* She's much better." Grace was holding something in her hands, a paper bag from the grocery store, but she seemed to have forgotten about it. "Thank you for the wildflowers you left on the front porch."

"Your *dat* shared that it's been a hard few nights."

"Indeed. I thought teething was difficult, but it's nothing compared to ear infections."

"You're certain Nicole is better?"

"I am. The second antibiotic that Doc Amanda sent out worked wonders."

Adrian crossed his arms and leaned against the wall of his barn. "I went to Doc Amanda when I was a child."

"So did I."

"Hard to believe she's still practicing."

"I know, right?"

"Whatcha got there?" He nodded toward the bag in her hands.

"Oh. This." She thrust it toward him. "I bought you something."

"For me?"

"Uh-huh."

He pulled out the pint of Ben & Jerry's. "Oh, man. This will hit the spot. Let me run inside and grab two spoons."

"Oh, I didn't mean—"

But Adrian didn't hear the rest. He ducked into his barn, jogged to the tiny kitchen at the end of his living area and snagged two spoons. By the time he made it back outside, Grace was sitting on the bench, her head back against the wall and her eyes closed.

"You must be beat."

She opened one eye and glanced at him, then shrugged and resumed her nap. The sun was nearing the horizon, and like during the walk they'd taken just a few nights before, it was dropping its rays across her. She reminded him of a cat sleeping in the sun, and he started to laugh.

"What's so funny?" Grace kept her eyes closed and her face tilted upturned toward the sun.

"Just thinking how you remind me of a cat, in more ways than one."

"Is that so?"

"Sure. You're sleeping in the sun."

"It's comfortable here. And quiet."

He sat beside her, placed the bag between them on the bench and the ice cream on top of the bag. "If you're cross with someone, you tend to hiss."

"I do not hiss." She didn't look at him, but now she was smiling, too.

"And you take care of Nicole with as much love and attention as our old barn cat used to take care of her litter."

"I don't know whether I should feel complimented or offended."

"Oh, it's a compliment, for sure and certain." He popped the top off the pint, stuck a spoon in and took the first bite. "Mmm, so rich and creamy. Don't you want some?"

"Ice cream is probably the last thing I need. All that sugar will keep me awake when I need to go home and sleep."

"The second bite is even better than the first."

"Though now that you mention it…" She sat up and accepted the spoon he was holding out to her. The expression on her face after the first bite was pure bliss.

"There's a reason it's my favorite."

"I've never had… What is this again?"

"Salted Caramel Almond. Hey, wait. How'd you just so happen to have a pint of my favorite ice cream?"

Now she shifted uncomfortably on the bench and was suddenly completely focused on digging out one more spoonful.

"Grace, did you buy this just for me?"

She put a huge spoonful in her mouth. "Can't talk. Mouth full."

"You did buy it for me. Just the other night we were discussing how I didn't have a freezer, and I said—"

She licked the spoon clean, reminding him again of a cat. Finally, she glanced at him and smiled. "You said that you loved Salted Caramel Almond."

"I can't believe you remembered."

"When Nicole first started running a fever, and I was so worried, all I could think of was getting her well." She dug out another spoonful, ate it, then stood, brushed her apron smooth, and finally looked at him. "Mamm had given me this wad of money from our emergency jar. That's a jar that we—"

"I know what an emergency jar is, Grace. My family has one, too."

"As I was leaving Doc Amanda's office and paid the bill, then went to pick up the medicine, I realized what a blessing it was not to have to worry about money at a time like that."

"You don't ever have to worry about money. Any number of people from our church will help if you need it, including myself."

"I realize that's probably true."

"It is true." He'd finished the pint of ice cream. He

set it on the bench next to their spoons. And that simple sight, two spoons next to an empty pint of ice cream, reminded him of what James Troyer had said earlier.

What was he waiting for?

Did he need to look at the woman standing in front of him in a different light?

"So when I went by the store to get her prescription— this was the first prescription, the pink medicine, which didn't help Nicole much—I thought of you."

"You thought of me?" He stood and stepped closer.

Instead of stepping back, she glanced up at him and smiled. It was maybe the first easy smile he'd seen from her. Maybe that was what exhaustion did—helped you to drop all pretenses.

"Well, *danki*. That was very kind."

"But I ate half of it," she teased.

"Maybe a quarter."

"Okay, a third."

"Guess we'll have to buy another." He moved beside her, and they both turned to look at the colorful display in the sky to the west.

"We have a habit of watching sunsets together."

"You can bring me ice cream anytime." He bumped his shoulder against hers, wishing he was brave enough to reach for her hand.

At that very moment, Triangle jogged around the corner, holding a squirrel in his mouth.

"Ew."

"Just bringing us a gift." Adrian picked up a dustpan leaning against the wall of his barn, then squatted down in front of the dog. "Good boy."

Triangle dropped the squirrel into the dustpan, then

flopped onto the dirt, panting and looking for all the world as if he was quite pleased with himself.

"Guess I need to dispose of this. If you're not too tired…"

"*Nein*, I've been trapped inside for four days."

"…want to go with me? We can stop and pet Cinnamon."

"I can think of nothing I'd like to do more than pet your camel."

Which was how they ended up walking across his place, on a perfect spring evening, as the sun set on another day.

Adrian wasn't thinking about animals or ice cream or even whether or not he should reach for Grace's hand. Instead, he was thinking of what her father had said.

The right time is now. As for the right person, that's often someone you just have to look at in a different light.

Which really left him with only two questions.

Was he falling for Grace Troyer?

And if he was, what was he going to do about it?

Chapter Seven

The next day was the first time in a week that Nicole finally acted like her old self. She smiled when Grace first went in her room, ate all of her breakfast and squealed with delight when Kendrick the Llama paused in his daily run to look in their kitchen window.

Grace felt good about leaving her *doschder* with Adrian's *schweschder* Lydia, and the evening's tour group was one of their most enjoyable yet. Now that she wasn't working against Adrian, against the tour's success, she could actually enjoy planning and preparing each meal. It was fun to cook for *Englischers* who claimed that Grace's homemade bread was wonderful and the fresh cheese they bought from down the road tastier than any they'd ever had before.

Grace was limited only by what she could serve in a picnic setting. She had a lot of ideas, and suddenly a part of her was once again that young girl who'd dreamed of being a chef. Moreover, she didn't have to skimp on ingredients because she had the money to spend and she knew that she'd more than earn it back.

Nicole plopped down, clapped her hands and hollered, "Lydee," when she saw Adrian's *schweschder*.

Her *mamm* once again sold another dozen items, further depleting her inventory.

Everything was going well. It made no sense that she woke on Friday restless and out of sorts.

"Your mood is probably caused by our beautiful weather."

"Shouldn't the weather make me feel better?"

"Not when you've been stuck in this house for a week."

"*Gut* point."

"I heard Adrian say he was going to be working in his vegetable garden. Why don't you go and help him? You could take Nicole with you. Some time outside would do you both good."

Grace knew that she could go out and work in their own garden, but perhaps her *mamm* was wanting some time alone. She could certainly understand that. So she packed a sippy cup and snack for Nicole, grabbed an old blanket, put on Nicole's lavender sweater and *kapp*, then tucked everything—including her *doschder*—into the stroller. They'd have to go down the lane and around by the road, but perhaps the walk was just what she needed.

And her mood did improve as she made her way over to Adrian's place. She found him on his knees in the garden next to the barn. Or what might have been a garden. It was hard to tell, with all the plants scattered around.

"What happened?"

"Hey." Adrian smiled up at them, blocking the sun with a hand. "I didn't hear you come up."

"What happened to your vegetables?"

"Ah…" He turned to survey the torn-up plants and demolished rows. "Goats."

"But…it's fenced. How'd they get in here?"

"I guess I left the gate open. I hear I should fix the latches on my gates."

There wasn't much she could say to that, since she'd definitely been a bad example to the very same goats. So instead of chiding him, she laid the blanket out under the shade of a nearby tree, plopped Nicole onto it and scattered a few toys around her.

"I'll help."

If Adrian was surprised, he hid it well. Within a half hour, they had a good amount of the vegetables replanted, though she wasn't entirely sure if they'd survive.

"Why don't they eat them, once they pull them up?"

"There's no understanding a goat. My only guess is they have a short attention span."

It felt good to work her fingers in the soil, and Grace realized that it was nice to be somewhere different. She spent entirely too much time on her parents' farm. Perhaps she should start going into town once a week.

Or maybe she needed friends.

That was probably it.

"You're focusing awfully hard over there."

"*Ya*. Just thinking that it feels good to be away from our place for a little while."

"I remember feeling that way when I was still staying at my parents' farm."

"You did?"

"Sure. I guess it's something about living in the same place after you're grown."

"Well, I might as well get used to that, because I'm not moving anywhere anytime soon." Grace glanced over at

Nicole, who was still happily sitting on the blanket, playing with her toys. Usually she'd be scrambling about, but the recent illness seemed to have left her with less energy. Or perhaps it was getting close to nap time. "Baby girl will be raised in the same house I was."

"You don't know that."

"Pretty much, I do."

"So you're saying you'll never marry?"

Grace had been tenderly replanting a tomato plant that had been ripped up by its roots. She sat back on her ankles and studied him. "I'm not sure that marriage is in my future, Adrian."

"Because of Nicole?"

"Because of her…and other things."

"Oh. Well, a wise man once said to me—"

"What wise man?"

"Your *dat*."

"Oh?"

"He said something to the effect that we need to stop waiting for the right time."

Grace suddenly wished the ground would open up and swallow her. Could things get more embarrassing? Was her *dat* actually pushing Adrian to date her?

"We?"

"And then he said that sometimes we just have to look at someone we already know in a different light."

"Adrian, I am mortified."

"Why would you be?" He looked at her quizzically, as if he didn't understand her embarrassment. Then he did something she did not expect. He tipped his hat back and started laughing.

"I fail to see what's so funny."

"Come on, Grace. It's not unusual for Amish parents

to push their single children into dating. You're aware of that, I'm sure."

"My parents haven't even mentioned that they think I should date."

"Maybe they're giving you time because of Nicole."

"About that…"

"But any man would be blessed to have you for a *fraa*, Grace. As for Nicole… She's a sweet *boppli*. You shouldn't let your decision to raise your cousin's child keep you from dating."

Except Nicole wasn't her cousin's child, and Grace wasn't sure if now was the time or place to share that important fact with Adrian.

Did her parents truly think it was time for her to date? Were they ready for her to get out from underfoot?

Why would her *dat* say such a thing to Adrian, the one person Grace considered a friend?

Adrian was a *gut* person, but she didn't think he was ready to be a husband or a *dat*. It took only one look at his garden to see that. He couldn't even remember to close the gate. His family would starve! As for the animals… She looked up as Dolly settled a few feet from them. The red-rumped parrot squawked something unintelligible and then commenced preening herself.

Adrian actually responded with a similar squawk, then looked at Grace and smiled.

It would take a patient woman, indeed, to agree to live in Adrian's menagerie. It would take someone completely smitten with him!

She wished him the very best in finding a woman to set up housekeeping in his barn. Was Adrian looking for a *fraa*? She felt the sudden and painful loss of his friend-

ship like an ache in her stomach, which was ridiculous…
He was kneeling six feet from her.

But it would happen.

Eventually some woman would take a shine to Adrian
Schrock, and she'd lose the one friend she had in Goshen. What was the point in growing close to someone,
in developing real friendships, when life seemed to rip
them away? Wouldn't she be better off learning to be
happy alone?

She'd thought herself in love with Kolby, then he'd
vanished.

She'd finally learned to trust Adrian as a friend—
nothing more—but he, too, would one day be pulled
from her world. Her mood sank to even lower than it
had been earlier that morning. Tears stung her eyes, and
she vowed not to let them spill down her cheeks. What
was wrong with her? Why was she so emotional? And
would someone please tell her how could she learn to
rein in her feelings?

Adrian wasn't sure what he'd said to upset Grace, but
she'd gone suddenly quiet on him. She sat there patting
the dirt around a plant that she'd already finished with,
her head ducked so that he couldn't see her expression.
Her shoulders were hunched, and she reminded him of
a turtle that had gone into hiding.

Why?

What had happened while they were working in the
garden?

He waited for a few moments to no avail. Grace was
completely focused on tapping down the earth around
the plant.

Perhaps she needed a distraction from whatever was

bothering her. He moved over to her row, picked up a bell pepper plant and plopped it into the ground.

"I've decided to farm organically."

"Excuse me?" She looked up at him with an expression that suggested he was wearing his suspenders backward.

"Organic farming. Surely you've heard of it."

"I guess."

"I've decided to do it. I even visited the library and checked out a few books on the subject. Did you know there's an Amish man in Ohio who has founded an organization—?"

"Hang on." Grace had been kneeling in front of the plants, but now she sat down, her legs crossed like a child. "I know what organic farming is. You're saying that you don't plan to use any fertilizers or pesticides."

"*Ya.* That pretty much sums it up."

"But why?" She shook her head as if she needed to free it from a bothersome thought. "You have more work here with all these animals than any one man can possibly handle."

Kendrick picked that moment to dash down one of the rows of vegetables, sidestepping onto the plants. Adrian jumped up, shooed the beast out of the garden area and closed the gate. When he walked back over to Grace, she still hadn't moved and she certainly hadn't reset any more of his plants.

"Where were we?"

"I was helping you replant until I found out you're not going to fertilize, which means the plants won't grow, so why bother?"

"Of course they'll grow. Plants don't have to be drowned in chemical fertilizers. They just need the right balance of nutrition. Zook says so in his book. Did you know that eggshells worked into the soil can provide needed calcium?"

"Do you eat eggs? Because I don't see any chickens here."

"Well, not often. Mainly when I'm at my folks. But I could buy a few chickens, and then I'd have eggs to eat. I could save the shells and put them on my plants. It's not that difficult to figure out, Grace."

"What is wrong with using regular fertilizer?"

He glanced up at the sky, trying to remember what he'd read the night before, then snapped his fingers. "Mahatma Gandhi said something to the effect that a *gut* man is a friend of all living things."

"You're quoting Gandhi now?"

"What's wrong with that?"

"It has nothing to do with whether or not to use fertilizer." She crossed her arms in front of her chest. "Changing the subject doesn't prove your point."

"I'm not changing the subject and I don't have to prove my point. Fertilizers and pesticides are not natural."

"Not natural?"

"*Nein.* They're both made in a laboratory, not in a field. I don't want to put any of those chemicals on my plants."

"Do you want to eat?"

"Ha ha. *Gut* one. You made a joke there."

She stood and brushed dirt off the back of her dress. "Actually, I was serious. I think I should be going home now."

Adrian jumped up to follow her. "Why are you so peevish today?"

"Peevish?"

"Irritable?"

"I'm irritable?"

The look she gave him caused Adrian to wish he'd simply let her go without a word. Now she'd stopped, hands on her hips, staring him down—though she had to look up to do so, since he was taller than her.

He brushed his hands against his pants leg, unable to look her in the eye. Why did he suddenly feel embarrassed, like he needed to apologize? He hadn't done anything wrong. He'd only shared his own opinion about natural farming on his place. "I don't know what I said earlier to change your mood."

Instead of answering, she turned her head and stared out in the direction of his camel.

"And the organic farming—I was just making conversation. I thought you'd be interested, especially in light of Nicole and all."

"What does this have to do with Nicole?" She turned to face him and skewered him with a pointed look.

"I'd think you'd want to feed her *gut* food—food free of chemicals."

"You're saying I feed my child poison?"

Adrian had a sudden and overwhelming urge to go brush his camel. Cinnamon was always glad to see him, enjoyed his attention, and she never argued. But instead of walking away, he fumbled around, looking for an answer that would wipe the angry expression off Grace's face. "I didn't say you feed Nicole poison, but I guess you could see it that way."

"But your way—organic farming, which you've probably studied all of three days—is the right way?"

"Natural is better, yes." Now he felt his temper flaring. He liked Grace, and he liked it when things were smooth and comfortable between them, but right was right and wrong was wrong. Unfortunately, he decided to voice that thought. "Right is right whether you like it or not."

"What did you say?"

"I said right is right and wrong is wrong."

"Oh, Adrian." She closed her eyes, and an expression that resembled amusement passed over her face. When she opened her eyes, she stepped closer, and to his surprise, she put a hand on each of his shoulders. "I remember what it's like to be your age."

"I'm older than you."

"There was a time when I, too, was quite sure of myself."

"I can show you the book on organic farming." He shifted from one foot to the other, uncomfortable with how close she was and the look of pity in her eyes.

"There was a time when I was convinced that I knew what was right and what was wrong—a time when I had had no doubts." She shook her head in a mournful way, walked over to Nicole and set about picking up her things.

"If you know what's right, why would you doubt it?"

She didn't answer right away. Instead, she clasped Nicole closer, whispered in her ear, straightened her *kapp*, smoothed down her dress. Those things seemed to calm her. When she looked up again, the anger and frustration had been replaced by a calm certainty. She stuffed the bag of toys and the quilt into the back of the stroller, then added Nicole, who waved her arms at Adrian.

He waved back—and waited.

Finally Grace answered his question. "To doubt is

normal. We doubt because we're imperfect and we make mistakes. We doubt because life isn't that simple."

She searched his eyes for something, again shook her head as if she were sorely aggrieved, then she turned and hurried down his lane, back to her parents' farm. Adrian stood there, watching her retreating figure and feeling the loss of something that he didn't quite understand. He didn't know what had just happened. He certainly didn't know what he'd done to set her off, but he did understand that Grace was not talking about farming—or at least not only farming.

He felt a nudge on his shoulder and turned to look into Kendrick's eyes. He reached up and rubbed the llama between his ears, which was exactly what Kendrick wanted. He really should stick to animals. They at least made sense to him.

For the next hour, no matter how he tried, he couldn't keep his mind on the animals. He finished his chores, thinking the entire time about Grace's brown eyes—eyes that reminded him of cocoa and coffee and chocolate, all things he loved. He thought of Grace staring up at him. What had she been trying to tell him? He was still puzzled over that.

He walked outside and looked over at the Troyer farmhouse.

He should go over there now and talk to her.

Nein.

The last thing she wanted was to see him.

So instead of going next door, he hitched up his gelding, Socks, and headed out to George's place. He found his friend in the barn, having already finished dinner.

"Does Becca know you're hiding out here?"

"*Ya.* She understands I need an hour to myself."

"I imagine she's the one who could use some private time, what with six *kinner* to care for."

"Normally I would agree with you, but her *schweschder* who lives in Wisconsin is visiting for a few days. My being out here gives them plenty of time to chat." George drew a pipe out of his pocket and began packing it with fresh tobacco, something with a sweet scent to it. Once he had it going, he motioned outside. They settled in chairs under the barn's eave.

"I don't understand women." Adrian had meant to tip-toe up to the subject, but the words popped out as soon as they were seated.

"Any woman in particular?"

"Grace."

"Ah."

"What does that mean?"

Instead of answering, George motioned for him to continue, so Adrian did. He laid out the entire, inexplicable afternoon. With each detail, the smile on George's face broadened.

"I don't understand what you find so amusing."

"Youngies."

"Please. I'm twenty-five."

"Uh-huh, but in matters of courting, you're a bit behind."

"Thank you for the insight, though it's most definitely not what I need to hear today."

"You're out of sorts. Probably a full day of splitting wood will put you in a better frame of mind."

"You want me to split wood? It's almost May. I won't need wood for months."

"True, but it's something that requires your complete attention and uses up a bunch of nervous energy."

"I don't have nervous energy. What do I have to be nervous about? I didn't do anything." He forced himself to stop jiggling his leg.

George studied his pipe for a moment, then stood and said, "Walk with me."

Adrian had five *bruders* and five *schweschdern*. He was squarely in the middle of eleven children. He loved his family, but he'd never gone to his *bruders* for advice. They weren't close in that way. He felt closer to George than he did to his own family. Maybe that was normal. He wasn't sure, but he followed George across to the pasture fence, interested in what he was about to say.

"I've a mind to give you some advice about women, if you're interested in hearing what I have to say."

"Sure, *ya*, but just so we're clear, Grace and I are friends—only friends."

"Okay. Let's leave that alone for a minute."

Which was a rather odd thing to say, in Adrian's opinion. Before he could correct him, George was speaking again.

"Three things." He ticked them off on his fingers for emphasis. "Number one—it's not always about you."

"What's not always about me?"

"Anything. A mood. A look. A perceived slight. Maybe the baby was teething that day. Maybe she feels a little blue because something she was working on didn't turn out quite right."

"Last week, Grace was making a cake that she claims fell. You'd have thought someone died. I don't even know what that means. Cake is cake. Right? How can it fall?"

"Number two. Don't go too fast."

"Go where too fast?"

"For a man, things can be simpler." George pointed

to his field with the stem of his pipe. "Say you need to plow that field. You hitch up the team and plow it. Simple. But for a woman, there's more things to consider. Maybe she wants the vegetable garden planted, because she's worried about having enough vegetables to put back for winter. Maybe she was planning on going to town, but now she can't because you're in the field and there's no one to watch the *kinner*. Maybe—"

"Maybe she doesn't know a thing about organic farming."

"Whatever. The point is, step back and give her some time."

"Okay. That makes sense."

"Number three. Don't go too slow."

"Seems to contradict your second point, which was don't go too fast."

George nodded as if that was his intent—to contradict himself. "A man and a woman can start out as friends, but if you stay there too long, if you don't act on your feelings, then you can miss an opportunity to grow closer."

The sun was setting, splashing a kaleidoscope of colors across the sky. Adrian didn't understand how sunsets worked any more than he understood women. "I'm not saying I have those kind of feelings for Grace, but hypothetically…"

"Yes, yes, let's keep this hypothetical." George didn't laugh outright, but he looked as if he wanted to.

"How would I act on those feelings?"

"Hypothetically…" George grinned, then pushed on. "You could start by bringing her flowers, maybe help her with a chore or ask her out to dinner."

"I can't afford a dinner in town."

"Ice cream, then. Whatever. You're missing the point.

Show her your romantic intentions, because once you fall firmly in the friend category, it's hard for her to see you differently."

"But as I said, we are just friends."

"Now. But do you always want to be just friends? Or do you think that you might one day be interested…romantically…in Grace?"

"I hadn't thought that far ahead."

"Uh-huh. That's plain enough."

If anyone else had said it, Adrian would have been offended, but as they turned and walked back toward his buggy, Adrian realized that George was trying to help. At least he wasn't laughing at him—not outright. The entire thing was embarrassing enough.

He climbed up into his buggy and was about to close the door when George stayed it with his hand. "One more thing. In many ways, women want the same thing men do. They want to be appreciated, listened to and valued. They're different from us in some ways—maybe even in how they relate to the world, but they're also the same."

Adrian resisted the urge to drop his head into his hands. Different but the same? Don't go too fast, but don't go too slow? Where did the madness end? And why couldn't women be as easy to care for as animals?

Because that was one thing Adrian had realized in the midst of George's advice. He very much cared about Grace. He wasn't sure if it was only as a friend or something more, but he knew that when things weren't right between them, he felt unsettled.

Now he had some ideas for how to get things back on a solid footing.

At least he thought he did.

Chapter Eight

On Saturday, Grace made up her mind to stop thinking about Adrian. It wasn't as if she wasn't busy. She had a child to raise, tour dinners to plan and… And nothing.

That was it.

Those two things were the entirety of her life.

Maybe she'd start a new hobby. She could learn to knit. Unfortunately, she tended to purl when she was supposed to knit and knit when she was supposed to purl. She often lost count and had to frog things out, and when that happened, she might as well start over because she could not thread the stitches back onto the needle.

She could clean. She'd always been good at that.

Grace's *schweschder* had picked up Nicole for a playdate with her *kinder*, so Grace had the entire day to herself. She decided to give the kitchen a good solid cleaning. She started with the oven. The brown stuff on the bottom that she had to scrub off somehow reminded her of Adrian's garden.

So what if he wanted to organically farm?

That was his business, not hers.

In the same way it wasn't her business if he let his

animals wander through his vegetable garden to graze every day.

And living in a stinky old barn? That was his choice. None of it had anything to do with her.

The calendar in the kitchen declared it was the first of May. Wasn't May the best month of the year? She should take advantage of the fine weather, but instead, after finishing in the kitchen, she attacked the rest of the house as if it hadn't been properly cleaned since winter. She and her mother had already done the spring cleaning a month earlier, though that fact didn't slow her down one bit. She beat rugs, mopped floors, scoured the two bathrooms, even took the stiff outdoor broom to the front porch.

Fortunately, her *mamm* was too busy knitting scarves and mittens for the *Englisch* tourists to notice her frenzied energy, and her *dat* was busy out in the barn.

And where was she? Stuck at home, cleaning an already clean house.

Grace whacked at the cobwebs on the porch.

The first of May, and she was stuck at home because she had no social life at all.

Turning the porch rockers over, she knocked dust off the bottom.

Soon it would be summer, and what did she have to look forward to? More tours. More cooking. More cleaning.

Her life was an endless cycle of sameness.

It was at that unfortunate moment of self-pity that Adrian pulled into the driveway, his horse, Socks, tossing his head and his dog, Triangle, sitting up smartly on the front seat.

Adrian was the last person she needed to see today, especially after their argument the previous afternoon.

She almost fled inside, but hadn't she done that just the day before? She'd run off rather than deal with his stubborn tunnel vision.

She personally hated it in novels when the main character ran from the room. Grace did read the occasional novel that she borrowed from the library. Some Christian romances her *schweschder* passed on to her. Georgia was always scouring garage sales for books, which she purchased four for a dollar or a dime a piece. They did come in handy on those nights when Grace was teething and wanted rocking. One couldn't knit while rocking a baby, but one could certainly read.

In those stories, when the main character inevitably turned and fled for whatever reason, Grace always wanted to shout "stand your ground!" Perhaps it was time she followed her own advice.

Instead of getting out of the buggy, Adrian pulled it around in the circle, stopping so that he could hang his arm and head out the window and speak to her. "I was just headed to town."

"Okay." She aimed for nonchalant but wasn't sure she was pulling it off. Must be nice to be able to gallivant off to town whenever one felt the urge.

"I wondered if you needed anything."

That was considerate of him to ask. If there was one thing that Adrian was *gut* at, it was thinking of others.

"Or maybe you'd like to come along?"

She glanced down at her dirty clothes.

As if he could read her mind, Adrian added, "Triangle and I aren't in any hurry."

She needed to change, and she did want to go to town. Suddenly she could think of nothing she'd rather do than get off this farm for an hour. Now wasn't the time to be too proud to accept an invitation.

"Give me ten minutes." She dashed into the house, splashed some water on her face, tidied up her hair, re-pinned her *kapp*, changed into one of her three weekday dresses, then took it off and put on her Sunday dress, then took it off and put back on her weekday dress. The sunglasses at least made her look as if she were heading somewhere special. She snagged her purse and hurried to the kitchen to tell her *mamm* where she was going, but her *mamm* wasn't there.

Then she heard voices and looked outside to see her *mamm* petting Triangle.

"It really is amazing that he gets around so well."

"The vet said he was born this way, so I suppose it's all he's ever known."

Who else but Adrian would adopt a three-legged dog?

Five minutes later, they were headed down the lane and Grace's mood had lightened considerably.

"Why are you headed to town?"

He didn't answer right away. Finally, he turned to her and grinned. "No real reason. Guess I need some time away from my place."

"I can relate to that."

"Funny how you can love your home and still need time away."

"Exactly. I woke with so much excess energy that I was cleaning the bottom of rocking chairs."

"Wow."

"I know."

The sun was shining, the day was pleasantly warm, and Triangle now sat on the seat in between them, watch-ing through the front window with a smile on his face.

"Anywhere in particular you'd like to go?"

Suddenly Grace realized that she did want to go somewhere in particular. She wanted to stop by the fabric store and purchase material for a new dress for Nicole. She wanted to check in at the dry goods store to see if they had the yarn her *mamm* had ordered. She wanted to go by the library. She blurted all that out to Adrian in one long, rambling sentence.

"All *gut* ideas." Adrian smiled at her, then allowed Socks to accelerate into a nice trot.

Why had she mentioned the library? She didn't really need to look at one of their cookbooks. She had a dozen *gut* cookbooks at home that she'd been using for years. She'd like to browse through something new, though—not that recipes changed much. Still, it felt as if her cooking was in a rut, rather like her life. She suddenly—desperately—needed to cook something different for their tour group. As for Adrian, he probably wanted to check out more books on organic farming, but that didn't bother Grace as much as it might have the night before.

Because she was going to town on a beautiful spring Saturday.

She was free of all obligations for at least the next three hours.

And she was with a friend.

For now, all that was enough.

They spent the next couple of hours enjoying the day. Only once did Adrian throw out a crazy quote he'd read recently—this one by William Wordsworth. "The flower that smells the sweetest is shy and lowly."

"You have some strange reading material, Adrian."

"*Ya?* I guess I do." He glanced at her sheepishly.

Somewhere along the way, Grace was able to forget that she was a single *mamm* who didn't know what she was doing with her life.

When they were at the library, she used the computer to print off half a dozen recipes. Adrian sat beside her, looking up best habitat improvements for a camel.

As they stood in line to pay for the copies she'd made, Adrian nodded toward a shelf of books with a sign that read For Sale—Donations Accepted.

"I guess I could look for my *schweschder.*" In the end she chose three books—a picture book for Nicole, a historical romance with a picture of a castle on the front for Georgia and a murder mystery with a drawing of an Amish B&B on the cover for herself.

"Murder mystery? Should I be worried?"

She decided that she liked this more easygoing Adrian. As she thumbed through her purse for money to put in the donation jar, she saw that he'd tucked a slim volume under his arm. When he slipped his dollar in the jar, his hand touched hers, and Grace's heart set off into a gallop.

Then he smiled that goofy grin, and she relaxed.

He was a *gut* friend and a nice neighbor. That was all. Nothing more.

He went next door to the hardware store while she purchased material in the fabric shop. She bought a little extra, deciding that she could make a matching dress and apron for Nicole's baby doll. She glanced at fabric for herself, too, but she truly didn't need a new dress. That could wait. Maybe after a few more weeks of tours.

And there it was again.

The tours. She had extra money in her pocketbook because of the tours, because of Adrian.

When he stopped in front of the local ice cream shop, she insisted on paying.

Adrian chose peanut butter Oreo, and she picked blueberry cheesecake. They carried their cups of ice cream over to one of the picnic tables and sat beside each other. Triangle flopped down in the dirt, his eyes closed, though he cast a glance at them occasionally as if to say "a dog can hope."

She looked over at Adrian, then focused on her ice cream. The sun was warm on her face, and the ice cream was sweet with a splash of tartness. It tasted rich and creamy and good on her tongue. *"Danki."*

"For what?"

"Stopping by my house, asking me to come along, being pleasant company… Take your pick."

"I'm pleasant company?"

"Don't make a thing out of it."

"Wouldn't dream of it." But the smile on his face told her that he was inordinately pleased with the compliment.

She savored another bite, then said, "We get along pretty well as long as we don't talk about anything important."

"So that's the secret." Adrian paused, a spoonful of ice cream nearly at his mouth and a twinkle in his eyes. "I was wondering."

"It's true."

"Ya, I suppose." He shrugged, then bumped his shoulder against hers.

Grace popped another spoonful in her mouth. "We're both opinionated people is the problem."

"I'm not opinionated. I'm right."

"Lord, grant me patience."

Adrian laughed, then Grace laughed, and Triangle

opened both eyes as if his treat might soon be a real possibility.

"You're a different kind of guy, Adrian."

"Uh-oh. That doesn't sound so great. Let's go back to my being pleasant company."

"No, seriously. You are different. You think differently. You view life…differently."

"Is that bad?"

"*Nein*, but it will take a patient woman to marry you."

"Know anyone who fits that description?"

Grace scrunched her eyes as if trying to remember who might be patient enough to take on such a project. "I'm coming up blank. Maybe you haven't met her yet."

"And maybe I have. Sometimes we have to look at someone we already know in a different light."

"I still can't believe my *dat* said that to you."

"So you disagree?"

"*Nein*. I don't disagree. It's just… Well, I'm not in a place in my life to be thinking about such things." She'd reached the bottom of her cup but had left a few drops for the dog. "Is it all right to give it to him?"

"Milk has sugar, and dogs can't process sugar." He reached into his pocket and retrieved a dog biscuit, then put it into Grace's hand. "Give him this instead."

"You carry dog treats in your pocket?"

"Guilty as charged."

"No wonder he's so devoted to you."

Triangle sat up pretty as could be and cocked his head, waiting for Grace to offer the treat in the palm of her hand. Grace had always thought of dogs as farm animals, good for warning off intruders. Now that she thought about it, Triangle could do both of those things. Triangle hadn't let his disability hinder him.

When she offered him the treat, he politely took it from her, then lay back down and happily devoured it.

They finished their ice creams and tossed the cups in the trash can. Grace realized she wasn't ready for the afternoon to end. She was surprised to find she enjoyed Adrian's company so much—when he wasn't lecturing her about organic farming.

It occurred to her then that Adrian knew things. He had an inquisitive mind, and that wasn't necessarily bad. But when you lived alone, who did you share your ideas and thoughts with? She struggled with that herself. She didn't live alone, but often she felt her parents wouldn't be interested in what she had to say. Their worlds were very different.

Did they care that she'd noticed a small wrinkle near her right eye?

Or that it was two years ago during the first week of May that she'd met Nicole's father?

Or that Nicole had put her chubby little hands on Grace's face and patted her, then said *mine*? Okay, her *mamm* and *dat* would both be interested in that one.

The point was that Adrian had fewer people to talk to than she did—unless you counted Triangle or Kendrick or Dolly. That had to be lonely. Sometimes, when he came across as bossy or arrogant, maybe he was just eager to share an idea.

She thought of his admonition about not giving milk to dogs and smiled to herself.

"Care to share?"

"Share?"

"What you're smiling about."

"Oh…that." She shook her head, thinking there was no way she was going to share what she'd been mulling over. But then it occurred to her that she might as well. What did she have to lose? And it felt good to talk about things, even wayward thoughts that popped out of nowhere.

Perhaps that was what friendship was—the freedom to say what was on your mind. Grace knew that she could use a friend at this point in her life.

The question was whether she dared to open herself up to the man sitting beside her, whether she was willing to take that leap, whether she could risk her heart—because even friendships had the power to hurt and wound.

Her relationship with Kolby had started out as a friendship but then quickly morphed into something else. It had all happened so fast it had made her head spin. She could see that now. She'd never felt so abandoned or alone or unworthy as when she'd realized he'd left town without even a goodbye. He'd left, and she didn't even know where he'd gone. He'd left, and she'd been pregnant with his child.

Kolby had hurt her in ways that might take years to heal.

But it had already been two years. Maybe it was time that she moved past what had happened. Maybe it was time she took a risk and allowed herself to be a friend to someone else. It was frightening, but then being alone wasn't working out so well, either.

Perhaps today was the day to try something different.

Adrian had expected to be nervous around Grace or uncomfortable being alone with her or even anxious to get back to his animals. He hadn't expected to thoroughly enjoy himself. But that was what he'd done all afternoon. The whole reason that he'd thought to invite Grace

along to ride with him to town was because of something
George had said.

It's not always about you.

Perhaps her frustration the day before had not been
about him. Maybe she'd been annoyed with her life in
general. A few hours away from the farm tended to clear
the cobwebs from his mind, like Grace had been clearing
the cobwebs from the bottom of the rockers. When he'd
seen her doing that, he'd known that she would agree to
go with him. He'd known it was the right thing to do to
ask her to go.

Now they were in the buggy, headed back toward
home, and Adrian wished the afternoon could last a little longer.

Then he saw her glance at him and smile. So he'd
asked what that was about. She took her time mulling
over her answer. Finally she angled herself in the seat so
that she was facing him.

"I guess I was thinking that you're not necessarily
bossy or arrogant."

"Who said I was?"

"Oh, I don't know if anyone said it exactly, but someone sitting here in this buggy might have thought it."

Triangle whined and dropped his head to the seat.
Adrian and Grace started laughing at the same time.
When her laughter had died away, Grace fiddled with
her purse, zipping and unzipping it. "I was thinking that
it's just that you know things. You probably read a lot."

"Not much else to do on a farm once the chores are
done."

"But lots of people read, Adrian. They read the *Budget*, over and over, like my *dat*."

"Your *dat* is a smart guy. He always knows where to buy the cheapest hay or the best seed."

"Sure. I get that. But you read books like—" she reached toward the pile of packages on the floor of the buggy and retrieved his book "—*Self-Reliance and Other Essays* by Ralph Waldo Emerson. What is this even about?"

"Well, it's essays, which are—you know—shorter writings."

"I know what an essay is."

"I enjoy reading them before bed, because often I'm too tired to read for very long."

"Uh-huh. That makes sense, and maybe I've heard of Ralph Waldo Emerson in school… But that was a lot of years ago, and I've had quite a few sleepless nights since then." She tapped the side of her head. "I might have forgotten a few things."

"Emerson was a philosopher and writer and poet."

"When did he live?"

"Eighteen hundreds."

"Not exactly current stuff."

"I guess, but a lot of what he wrote about transcends the time he wrote it."

"Give me an example."

"Okay." Adrian rubbed his chin, a little surprised that Grace was interested in Emerson. But then why shouldn't she be? She obviously had an intelligent, curious mind. "Emerson believed that all things are connected to God, so all things are divine."

"Like that newly planted field." She nodded toward the west, where an *Englisch* farmer had recently planted his crops.

"Sure."

"Or animals."

"Exactly."

"Or even children."

"*Ya*. I'm not going to pretend I understand his philosophy, but I like to think about how our plain and simple life is connected to the divine, to *Gotte*'s work."

"See? That's what I'm talking about. You know stuff."

"A lot of what I know is useless. Trust me. For example, did you know that the word *camel* in Arabic means *beauty*?"

"I did not know that."

"Now you do."

"And every time I think of Cinnamon, I will now think of it and be reminded of how beautiful she is."

They were nearly to her house. Adrian's mind cast around for some way to postpone taking her down the lane, but he couldn't think of a single excuse. So he turned in, though he called out to Socks, slowing him down a bit.

"When you were telling me about organic farming, I thought you were being a show-off…"

"Not my intent."

"…and naive."

"Always a possibility."

"And then I thought you were judging the way that I'm raising Nicole."

He pulled to a stop in front of the house, next to the buggy that belonged to Georgia. Grace had shared that Georgia had picked up Nicole for a playdate. The fact that her *schweschder* had beat them home meant Grace would be eager to go inside to see her *doschder*. But what she'd said about him judging her… He needed to correct that impression.

Turning in the seat, he looked directly at Grace and fought the urge to reach out and cover her hands with his. He didn't want to ruin this day by being too forward, but neither did he want to go too slow. He settled for reaching forward with one hand and squeezing hers lightly, then letting it go.

"I think you're doing a fantastic job raising Nicole, and I'm amazed at what a kind and generous person you are to even do such a thing. Raising a child that isn't yours? That takes a special kind of person, Grace, and you are special. You're terrific, actually."

She glanced down at her hands, worrying her bottom lip, then began gathering her packages. Had he said something wrong again? Or was she just tired? When she looked up at him, her expression was more solemn. She started to speak, stopped, shook her head, then hopped out of the buggy.

"*Danki*, Adrian. I had a *wunderbaar* time."

And then she was gone, leaving him to wonder if he'd gone too slow or too fast or if maybe—finally—he'd managed to hit it just right.

He went home and checked on Cinnamon, then made sure the goats hadn't escaped their pasture. Triangle ran at his side. Adrian considered Triangle something of a wonder. When he'd first adopted the dog from the local shelter, he'd stopped by the vet he used for his other animals and asked for advice.

After assessing the area where Triangle's hind leg should have been, the vet had stood and smiled. "Looks to me like your dog was born with only three legs."

"It wasn't an amputation?"

"Nope. There's no scar there."

"Anything special I should do?"

"Keep his weight down. That's probably the most important thing. Exercise is good as is swimming, if you have a pond."

"Thanks, Doc."

"No problem." The vet had walked him out to the counter where a receptionist was waiting to print out Adrian's bill. "No charge today."

"I don't mind paying."

"And I'll be happy to take your money when you bring Triangle back in for his annual vaccinations."

"Danki."

"Thank you for taking a dog that some people would see as damaged. Many people would never have considered doing such a thing." The vet had clapped him on the back, tossed a dog bone to Triangle and gone back to work.

Many people would never have considered doing such a thing.

Those words circled in Adrian's mind as he walked his farm, then went inside and made a simple supper. Triangle flopped down in his corner of the kitchen, though really the room was too small to be called that. There was a sink, a half refrigerator, a small two-burner stove and a cabinet with a few dishes in it. He had what he needed.

It occurred to him that perhaps the reason that Grace wasn't dating was the same reason that no one had adopted Triangle. Perhaps no one had considered dating her.

Why wouldn't they?

Because of Nicole?

But in Adrian's mind, Nicole only made Grace more appealing. Nicole was evidence of what a caring, kind, selfless person Grace was. Oh, she had a temper, for sure. He'd seen that often enough, but who wanted a perfect *fraa*?

He choked on the bite of sandwich he'd swallowed, and Triangle raised an eyebrow as if to say, "you okay, boss?"

Was he thinking of marrying Grace?

They hadn't even gone on a proper date yet.

But they had shared an afternoon trip to town, and it had gone well. If that was any indication of her feelings for him, then he thought he had a chance.

Marriage was a long way off—if it was even a possibility.

He didn't have much to offer a *fraa*.

But dating was a different thing.

Dating was simply getting to know one another. He could do that. One didn't need a proper kitchen or a lot of money in the bank in order to do that.

Adrian realized he was ready to begin courting, and the one woman he was interested in just happened to live next door.

Chapter Nine

Grace often found herself dreading church, then feeling guilty for having such a bad, unspiritual attitude. The truth was that her conscience bothered her more than ever of late. She wanted to stand at the front of the assembled group and proclaim that Nicole was her *doschder*, but of course that sort of thing simply wasn't done.

During their new members' class, she tried to focus on Bishop Luke's words. He was instructing them about the *Ordnung*, their unwritten rules. The *Ordnung* guided their everyday life. It covered such things as the type of dress they wore. For example, when Grace was a small girl their local *Ordnung* had been changed to allow women's dresses to be made out of fabric with pastel colors—before that most dresses had been gray or dark blue or dark green. Someone wised up to the fact that pastels were a nice color, too, though of course, red and orange and purple fabrics were still out of the question. It wasn't that they thought bold colors were bad, only that they sought to be humble.

A more recent change to their *Ordnung* had been to allow the gradual adoption of solar power. Some *En-*

glischers saw that as hypocritical, since they didn't use electrical power. Amish didn't believe in being connected to the grid. They were supposed to live their lives separate, set apart. Could someone live set apart with electricity in their home? Possibly, but with that electricity would come many temptations—television, radio and even the internet.

Solar power, on the other hand, allowed them to be separate but with some of the conveniences of modern life. They still wouldn't have a television or a radio or a computer, but they would be able to charge their tools and batteries, possibly even hook their refrigerator and stove up to it. Solar power would be much simpler and cheaper than propane. Plus solar power was basically free once the panels were set up. The sun was a part of *Gotte*'s creation. The Amish saw it as using *Gotte*'s natural resources.

Personally Grace was in favor of pastel dresses and solar-powered generators. She didn't think putting Nicole in a lavender-colored dress would make her *doschder* overly proud, and she certainly didn't think there was anything wrong with a fan that used batteries charged by the solar-powered generator in their barn.

But it wasn't fabric or fans that Grace thought of as she sat through the prayers and sermons. Instead, she was wrestling with her need to bare her soul.

After the service, she helped in the lunch line. Although many of the women still gave her the cold shoulder, a few women were polite to her. Anna Lapp asked how Nicole's teething was going, but then before Grace could answer, she'd had to run and check on one of her *boppli*. Anna was the same age as Grace, but she'd married at eighteen and now had four *kinner*. Occasionally,

Grace thought they might be friends, but Anna didn't seem to have time for such things.

As for the other women, the ones who stopped talking when Grace walked by them, she was trying not to let them ruin her day. Perhaps they weren't even talking about her. Maybe they simply thought she wouldn't be interested in the topic of their conversation.

Or maybe *she* was the topic of their conversation.

There was nothing she could do about it either way.

Bishop Luke paused in front of where she was shuffling pieces of pie to the front of the table. "I hope you enjoyed the new-member class today, Grace."

"*Ya*, I did." She moved Nicole from her right hip to her left. "I'm looking forward to the baptism service."

"Excellent. And remember, if you need to, you're always welcome to bring Nicole to class with you."

But Grace knew that none of the other candidates would be bringing children. She'd learned the oldest among them was nineteen—a full four years younger than she was. Four years seemed like a lifetime to Grace. So instead of taking Nicole with her into the area where they had class each Sunday, she arranged for her *mamm* to look after Nicole while she was meeting with the other candidates.

Still, it was kind of the bishop to offer such a thing.

Or was he trying to tell her something else?

Was he suggesting that she confess her indiscretions to her other classmates?

She was stewing over the conversation when Adrian appeared in front of her. "Come and sit with us when you're done?" He nodded toward George and Becca Miller who were spread out around the far picnic table with their six children.

"Okay."

"I could take Nicole now, if you'd like."

Before Grace could answer, Nicole lurched toward Adrian, reaching as far as she could and calling out, "Aden, Aden, Aden."

Grace passed Nicole over the table to Adrian. It startled her how natural her child looked in his arms.

"She still can't say my name."

"Don't let it hurt your feelings. Half the time she calls me *mamama*."

Nicole turned in Adrian's arms, pointed at Grace and said, "Mamama."

"See what I mean?" She pushed a piece of apple pie toward Adrian. "Take that with you. She loves apple."

As he walked off with her baby girl, it occurred to her that Adrian would make a *gut dat*. He really should settle down, find a *fraa* and start a family.

Where had those thoughts come from?

Just because he'd taken her to town the day before did not mean he was interested in courting. It also did not mean that he would want a ready-made family.

Grace stayed at the serving table until most of the desserts were gone, then grabbed an empty plate, forked a piece of ham on it, added a spoonful of beans and a piece of fresh bread, and hurried over to where Adrian and his friends were sitting.

She expected to be uncomfortable.

She didn't really know George and Becca Miller that well.

But she found she enjoyed sitting with Adrian's friends and hearing stories about him.

"I mostly hung out with Adrian's older *bruder*." George pushed his plate away and crossed his arms on the table. "Adrian insisted on hanging around the big boys, which used to drive Joseph crazy."

"Grace probably doesn't remember my older *bruder*." Adrian was still holding Nicole. He turned her in his arms so that she was facing the table. Then he handed her a spoon and she proceeded to try to pick up Jell-O and eat it. About one in three times, the jiggly red snack made it into her mouth. "Joseph is ten years older than me, same as George."

"Are you calling me an old man?"

"*Ya.* Come to think of it, I am." Adrian wiped off Nicole's face. "Anyway, Joseph moved to Maine. Left George here to look after me."

"Which is a full-time job, I can tell you." He proceeded to tell how Adrian had decided to turn a cattle trough into a fish tank when he was ten years old. "By the time Joseph figured out what Adrian was doing, the cattle could barely drink out of it, the thing was so full of fish and turtles."

The men turned the conversation to farming, and Becca and Grace talked about children and the coming summer break. "Only two of mine attend this year. But the middle two will start year after next. Then I'll have some time alone with the babies."

Grace couldn't imagine having six children. Some days, she was completely worn-out with just one.

She enjoyed sitting with Becca and George. Even though they were older, she felt she had more in common with them than she did with the girls her age. And she liked learning about Adrian's antics.

They were walking down by the creek, just Grace and Nicole and Adrian, when she stopped and studied him. "Why don't I remember any of the things George was talking about? We've always gone to the same church, attended the same school…"

"Maybe you have a terrible memory."

She reached out and pushed him. He laughed and put a hand on her elbow, tugging her toward an old rope swing that the older children had ignored in lieu of a game of baseball.

"It's probably because I'm older than you."

"Only two years."

"When you're in school, two years seems like an awful lot."

"I guess. I feel like I should have paid attention better." What would her life have been like if she'd given the time of day to someone like Adrian rather than falling recklessly in love with Nicole's father? But each time regret crossed her mind, she was brought up short. She couldn't make herself wish away the mistakes of her past, not when she looked at Nicole.

They were walking under a stand of trees. Grace glanced up, then looked over at Adrian.

"What?"

"Nothing."

"I suspect it's something."

"Don't you have a quote to share…about the trees?"

"Hmm, let me think." He rubbed his forehead for a few seconds, then snapped his fingers. "I've got it."

"Wordsworth again?" She was teasing him, but actually she was curious.

"Blake."

"As in William Blake, the poet?"

"The same." Adrian pointed to a tall maple tree, growing off by itself. "Blake said that a fool doesn't see the same tree as a wise man."

"Huh."

"You asked for a quote."

"So it all depends on the eye of the beholder?"

"Maybe. If you're a tree."

Laughing, they walked over to the maple tree with the old rope swing. Adrian nodded toward it and grinned. "Have a seat."

"There?"

"Sure."

"Why?"

"I'll push."

"You'll push me and Nicole?"

"I'm strong. I can handle it."

"Uh-huh. I guess the bigger question is whether the rope can handle it."

The rope held, and she found herself laughing as Adrian pretended to struggle with their weight. The rope creaked and the breeze cooled Grace's brow. Nicole laughed and clapped her hands. It was a rare moment of delight as Grace let go of her worries and stepped, for a moment, outside the endless circle of thoughts that plagued her.

As the afternoon progressed, it became obvious to Grace that Adrian was interested in courting, and she found herself warming to the idea.

True, it made her a bit nauseous to think of letting someone close. Perhaps the fluttery feeling in her stomach should make her run the opposite direction, but then she'd watch Adrian interact with Nicole and her doubts would melt away. Surely a man who could be so kind to a child wouldn't break her heart?

Because that was one of the things that scared her. It had taken her nearly two years to recover from Kolby's rejection. He hadn't rejected Nicole, not really, because he didn't know about her. He was long gone by the time Grace had realized she was pregnant.

How many months had she spent praying he'd come back?

Had she done something wrong, something to drive him away?

Or had he never really cared about her to begin with?

And which was worse?

Adrian and Nicole were pulling wildflowers from the fence line when Grace pulled her attention back to the present. Nicole looked up at Adrian and pushed the flowers toward his nose. Adrian laughed at Nicole's insisting, "Smell, Aden. Smell." Then he looked up at Grace, and in that moment, another part of the ice she'd carefully constructed around her heart began to melt.

Maybe it was time she took a chance.

Maybe it was time for her to trust what her heart was trying to tell her.

Adrian wanted to kiss Grace.

And yet…he didn't.

He was still thinking about George's advice—*don't go too slow, don't go too fast, listen.*

Her parents had gone home while Grace was playing volleyball. He'd never seen her play any game. He'd never seen her so relaxed. He was holding Nicole on the sidelines, cheering on Grace's team, when her parents walked up, looking for their *doschder.*

"I'm happy to give Grace and Nicole a ride home."

Grace's *mamm* thanked him, then sent a knowing look to her *dat.* Perhaps Adrian wasn't being as subtle as he thought he was. He didn't much care. It didn't bother him one bit if people knew that he had feelings for Grace or that he adored Nicole.

When the game was over, Grace collapsed in the grass beside him.

"I should probably get more exercise."

Her hair was sneaking out from the sides of her *kapp*, her face was flushed and sweat glistened on her forehead. In other words, she looked prettier than ever.

It was later, when he was taking her home, that he started thinking about kissing her. Nicole had fallen asleep in Grace's lap. She was curled there, in the last of the day's light, a look of complete relaxation on her face. Why was it that only children slept with such abandon? Adrian kept glancing at them, thinking how glad he was that he'd purchased the farm next to Grace's parents.

Thinking of how good Grace would feel in his arms.

Thinking that he'd been lonely before, maybe for years, but he hadn't realized it.

He wanted to kiss her, but he also realized this was probably one of those moments when he shouldn't go too fast. Grace had spent the entire afternoon with him, and she'd done so in front of all of their church members. That was a big step for her. He was learning that she was a very private person, and also very careful.

So instead of kissing her when he pulled up in front of her house, he set the brake and turned to face her.

"I had a *gut* time today."

"We did, too. *Danki* for, well, for everything."

"I have a question for you, if that's okay."

"Of course." Her eyes widened when he reached for her hand.

He laced his fingers with hers, satisfied at the sight of their hands intertwined. Pulling in a deep breath, he gathered his courage and looked into her beautiful brown eyes. "I care for you, Grace. For you and Nicole. I was wondering… That is, I'd like to ask if—"

She waited, but she didn't look away and she wasn't shaking her head no. He took those as good signs.

"I'd like to court you, if that's okay. If you'd like me to."

She didn't speak for a moment, and then she reached out with her other hand and touched his face. "I'd like that."

"You would?"

"*Ya.*" She pulled her hand away, a look of concern shadowing her smile. "But here's the thing, Adrian."

She glanced down at Nicole, kissed her on the head, then looked up and met his gaze. "Nicole cares about you."

"I care about her."

"In my mind, she thinks of you like an *onkel*—a favorite *onkel*."

"That's *gut*, right?"

"*Ya*, but if this doesn't work, if during our courting we find out that we're not right for each other… I don't want Nicole to lose her favorite *onkel*."

"That's not going to happen, Grace." His voice grew husky at the thought of not being a part of Nicole's life, of Grace's life. He'd only recently admitted how much they brightened his day. He couldn't begin to imagine losing them now. They would be taking a risk by pushing their relationship toward something else. But it was a risk worth taking, and he only needed to convince Grace of that in order for them to move forward. He did understand Grace's worry. What she was saying was about herself as well as Nicole. "We'll always be *gut* friends. You have my word on that."

"Okay." She looked as if she wanted to believe him. "I better get her inside."

He wanted to see her to the door, but she was already struggling out of the buggy, carrying a sleeping Nicole. She hurried up the porch steps, and in the last of the day's light, she turned and waved.

Adrian didn't remember driving home. The next thing he knew, he was standing in the aviary, putting seed into the finch feeder. Triangle had followed him into the birdhouse, and Kendrick was camped outside the door, waiting for his evening snack.

He thought about how not so long ago, Grace had shown up in the aviary, brandishing a rolling pin. She'd been so determined to not be a part of the tours. She'd been so afraid, and he still wasn't sure of what. But she was calmer now. She was on board with the plan to host *Englischers*, and they'd even discussed expanding to an extra tour day. Business-wise, things were going very well.

Who would have thought that they'd end up courting? It sounded like something from the romance novels his youngest *schweschder*, Lydia, occasionally read. In other words, it sounded improbable, but it also felt like *Gotte*'s planning.

All Adrian had to do, if you looked at it that way, was not mess things up.

He spent that night creating a list of improvements he'd like to make around his farm.

Build and install a swing for Nicole. There was a perfect place under the maple tree next to the camel pen. *Reinforce the fencing around the garden.* Maybe even add a few more plants. *Ask Mamm how to put the vegetables up for winter.*

Build a house.

He tapped his pen against the pad of paper, then circled the fourth item. That was the crucial thing. If Grace did fall in love with him, if they decided to marry, he couldn't ask her to live in a barn. The home could be small, but there needed to be space to add on to it. He knew the perfect spot. The drive into his property angled off to the right, where the barn and animal pens were located. But he could grade another drive to the left, where there was a good half acre of land surrounded by trees. It sat up on a small rise and afforded a good view of the rest of the property.

He'd once thought of turning it into a pasture for miniature horses, but horses were happy wherever you put them, as long as they had grazing, a little shade and a trough for water.

But a house needed to be somewhere special.

Because that was where he'd spend the rest of his life with his *fraa* and where they'd raise their children.

But how would he manage to build a house while he was just getting his business off the ground?

How could he afford it?

He didn't bother tallying up the costs. If they decided to marry, he knew a work crew would show up to help build a home. Hopefully he could save enough to pay for the supplies.

He could do that with the tours, especially if they added another day.

Was he thinking way ahead? *Ya.* He was, but it was better than not thinking things through at all, which, if he was honest, had been his mode of operation the last few years. That wasn't good enough for Grace or Nicole, though. He needed to anticipate their needs and be ready with solutions.

Because he cared about them.

He picked up his Bible and turned to where he'd been reading the night before—Proverbs. Solomon was always a *gut* read. "Ponder the path of thy feet, and let all thy ways be established."

Ponder the path of thy feet.

He stared at the page, thinking about how he needed to take more time to do that. Finally his thoughts turned to the look of vulnerability on Grace's face when she'd brought up what might happen if their courting didn't work out. Had she courted before? Had her heart been broken? And now she had to think not just of herself but also of Nicole.

Court Grace.

Spend time with Nicole.

Begin saving for a home.

Those things were more important than his other list. They also seemed pretty simple to him. The only question was what he would do if their courting didn't work. Because he already cared about both Grace and Nicole, more than he would have thought possible. Since he was being honest with himself, it was time to admit that he couldn't imagine his life without them. Even considering such a thing caused sweat to bead up on his brow.

Life without seeing Grace's smile?

Days without hearing Nicole's laugh?

Nein.

That just wasn't possible, so he needed to commit himself fully to winning her heart. The time had come to show Grace how much he cared.

Chapter Ten

The next week flew by for Grace.

On Monday, she took Nicole in for her vaccinations and well-baby visit. Doctor Amanda assured her that Nicole was doing fine in every category.

She was a little ahead in her speech and where she should be as far as grasping objects, walking, even feeding herself.

"Though, more lands on the floor than in her mouth," Grace said.

Doc Amanda smiled. "Every new mother should have a dog to clean up those messes."

Grace thought of Triangle. Nicole loved Adrian's dog, though she'd yet to master his name. It still came out "Angle," but the little dog never failed to make her *doschder* smile.

Nicole's weight was squarely in the middle of the chart.

Her height was below average, but then Grace was only five foot three.

"And her father?" The doctor smiled as she asked, adding another notation on the computer tablet.

"A little taller. I don't know exactly how tall."

The doctor glanced up at her, cocked her head, then set the tablet aside. She was sitting on her little stool that rolled easily around the exam room, and now she scooted closer to the wall, rested her back against it and focused on Grace.

"You're not the first mom to be a single parent, Grace." When Grace only shrugged, the doctor added, "I have at least three children under my care right now—all of them are being raised by single moms."

"Are they Amish children? Are they Amish single moms?"

"No. They're not. Which isn't to say that I haven't had other single moms who were. You have to remember I've been in this community a long time. This isn't a new issue."

"It's definitely new in my family."

"You live with your parents?"

"Ya."

"And how are they reacting to having you and Nicole in their home?"

"Gut. My parents are great, actually. They don't… don't want to talk about what happened before, but they've been very supportive since we moved back." Tears pricked her eyes as she added, "They're kind to me, and they adore Nicole."

Nicole looked up at her name. She'd been playing with a toy the doctor had handed her to test her dexterity skills. Holding up one of the plastic animals that looked like a llama, she said, "Kendrick," and then she plopped it into the correct hole.

Both Grace and the doctor laughed, though Doc Amanda couldn't have known about Adrian's llama.

"I'm happy to hear things are going well with your parents." The doctor picked up her tablet and walked to the door, but she paused and turned back, her hand on the doorknob. "Just remember, the way life is today isn't the way life is always going to be."

And then she was gone, leaving Grace to wonder just what she had meant by that parting statement. But of course she knew. As she drove back to her parents', she wondered if she believed it.

Life was a bit lonely now. Would it always be?

Certainly it was hard at times. Could she hope it would get easier?

And if she were honest with herself, occasionally the future stretched out like a road that continued forever in the distance, never deviating left or right, up or down, just an endless line of sameness—laundry and dishes, cooking and sewing, six days of work followed by a day of rest where she didn't quite fit into any group.

Did she see her life changing for the better?

Adrian believed it was possible.

At times, he seemed naively optimistic to her, as if you could decide a thing and it would just happen. Purchase a farm and turn it into your life's dream. Build a zoo and the animals would come. Fall in love and walk off into the sunset together.

Grace wanted to believe in those things, but it was frightening to get her hopes up. It was actually quite terrifying to allow herself to care again. What if everything went south? She probably wouldn't be any worse off than she had been when she was alone and pregnant, but she didn't want to once again endure that sort of pain. It had been too hard to recover the last time.

Sometimes, feeling nothing was better than making her heart vulnerable.

She just didn't know if she was brave enough to risk that kind of disappointment and rejection again.

What she did know was that when she was with Adrian, life seemed better. The burdens she carried around on her shoulders seemed a bit lighter.

Was that love?

Monday gave way to Tuesday, and she found herself looking forward to the tour guests.

For Tuesday's dinner, she made Swiss Mushroom Chicken and corn fritters, with a fresh salad and blackberry cobbler. There were no leftovers to put up. On Thursday, she cooked bacon-ranch pasta salad with grilled ham sandwiches, and peanut butter fingers for dessert. Several of the women claimed they'd love to buy a cookbook if she had one. Grace had found the recipes in the book from the library, but she'd swapped out a few ingredients and adjusted a few others.

Could she write a cookbook?

How would she even do such a thing?

She would ask Adrian's opinion on Saturday. He would be honest with her, and he was good at weighing the pros and cons of something—though he always tilted toward the pros. He was taking her out to dinner, and her *mamm* had insisted on watching Nicole.

"It's hard to court if you take your child with you."

"But we're a package deal—me and Nicole."

"Of course you are, but trust me, time alone is important for every couple, whether you've just met, are courting or are married. Plus baby girl and I could use some girl time."

"Hey. I'm sitting right here," Grace's *dat* chimed in.

Which caused Nicole to toddle over to her *daddi*, who scooped her up, then set her on his lap and proceeded to read to her from the *Budget* in funny voices, as if it were a children's book.

Adrian had spoken with Grace and her parents about adding more tour dates. They agreed that it needed to be a unanimous decision, made by all involved with the tours. So they scheduled a meeting for Friday afternoon at four o'clock. Grace baked oatmeal bars, made raspberry tea and brewed a fresh pot of coffee. She had never hosted a meeting before, but she was as ready as she was going to be. Adrian's idea to expand to Saturdays sounded good on the surface. In theory, if they went from two tours a week to three, they could increase their profits by 50 percent. But there were still only seven days in a week, and giving up another day might be hard on some of their group. It was best to address all concerns up front.

Old Saul showed up for the meeting fifteen minutes early, which wasn't a problem because he immediately fell into a deep discussion about cows with her *dat*. Seth arrived next, claiming he could barely find the place without a buggy full of tourists. He joined the men out on the porch. Then George Miller arrived, representing the Goshen Plain Tourism Committee. Her *mamm* and *dat* were also sitting in on the meeting. Which left only Adrian. Where was he?

By 4:15 p.m., even her *mamm* was concerned. "Perhaps you should go check on him."

"*Ya. Gut* idea."

Nicole was sitting in her high chair, eating a snack of Cheerios, though a good portion of them were falling to the floor. Grace thought of what the doctor had said, about how it helped to have a dog to clean up such messes. She had to admit it would be helpful to have Triangle there to scoop up the fallen bits.

Yes, that was exactly what she needed—a house dog.

She was probably going a little crazy.

Too much pressure. Too many changes.

But she didn't feel crazy or under pressure, and she was enjoying the changes.

It finally felt like her life, which had been on hold for so long, was moving forward again.

She hurried over to Adrian's. He wasn't in the aviary, and though she knocked on the barn door, no one answered. She even stuck her head inside the barn and shouted, "Yoo-hoo! Anyone home?" All to no avail.

He had to be home. Socks was out grazing in the pasture.

She found him with Cinnamon, holding one of the camel's hooves between his legs and brandishing a large metal file that he was using to grind down her nails.

"What are you doing?"

"Oh. Hi, Grace. I didn't hear you come up."

"What are you doing?" she repeated, her voice rising. When he looked at her blankly, she wanted to shake him. "Did you forget about the meeting?"

He dropped his head, though he still held on to the camel's hoof. "*Ya.* I guess I did."

"Everyone is at my place—waiting."

"Right. Okay. I'll just finish this and—"

"Adrian! Now. You need to come over now." She felt the beginnings of a headache in her left temple. She tried to rein in her frustration, but she was comfortable with Adrian now. It was difficult not to share what was bothering her, and why should she hold back? He was the one who had called the meeting, and now he'd forgotten?

"Adrian, how could you?" Her hands went to her hips of their own accord, as she squinted her eyes at him. "This was your idea. I made snacks. I cleaned up the house. I even changed my apron. Now you need to get over there and lead this meeting!"

Adrian's eyes widened, but instead of becoming defensive, he grinned at her. "You're cute when you're angry."

"Don't."

"Gives you a little blush to your cheeks."

"Teasing me won't change a thing. I'm still aggravated." But in truth, her heart was racing from the way he was looking at her, and he seemed to have forgotten he was holding Cinnamon's hoof.

"I have a sudden urge to kiss you."

"Here? In the middle of Cinnamon's pen?" Now her face, neck and ears felt impossibly hot. He'd inadvertently hit on something she'd been thinking about—what it would be like to kiss Adrian Schrock. Instead of giving in to the embarrassment, she tossed her *kapp* strings over her shoulders. "You want this to be our first kiss?"

He was at her side in three long strides. And suddenly she didn't care about tour dates or visitors or the fact that Cinnamon was staring at them curiously.

He slipped a hand to the back of her neck, tilted her face up to his and kissed her softly on the lips once, twice, then a third time. When he stepped back, the smile on his face made her laugh.

He looked like a child on Christmas morning.

He looked like she felt.

Had she fallen in love with this man? The man who

forgot meetings and allowed his goats to pillage his garden and quoted poets? None of that mattered, though. Not really. His shirt was covered with pieces of straw, dirt and camel hair. His pants weren't in any better shape, and his hair looked as if he'd forgotten to comb it.

He was a mess!

So why did Grace's heart lighten as he hurried back down the lane with her?

Honestly, she didn't care if his clothes were dirty— that was part of the life of being a farmer.

As for his hair, if she could get him to sit still, Grace's *mamm* could give him a *gut* haircut. Her *mamm* had been cutting her *dat*'s hair for as long as Grace could remember.

They found everyone assembled on the back porch, enjoying Grace's oatmeal bars and cold drinks. Only Seth seemed particularly put out that they were starting late. "I need to get home and clean up," he explained. "I'm taking Lynda Beachy to the Art in the Park Festival. They're having food trucks, music, even balloons and such for the kids. You should take Nicole, Grace. She'd love it."

"She goes to bed pretty early."

"It's running all weekend, eight in the morning to nine at night."

Adrian winked at her, then said, "Great idea, Seth. Now, let's get you out of here in time for your date."

As Adrian laid out their plan, everyone nodded in agreement. Grace was surprised when every single person was in favor of adding a third day. She'd thought that perhaps they'd be too busy with their various jobs and families.

Old Saul said it made no difference to him or his cows.

Seth said he certainly didn't mind driving another

day. "The tips are *gut*, and my buggy horse enjoys the opportunity to show off."

Surprisingly, only her mother voiced any concern at all. "I can't keep up with the demand for my knitted items as it is. They're buying everything I make, which is a *gut* problem but still a problem."

George leaned forward, elbows propped on knees. "Leslie brings up an important point. Growth is something that has to be managed in the tourism market. It's *wunderbaar* that things are going so well with you all, but at the same time, you don't want the quality of the experience you offer to suffer."

He turned to Grace. "Are you sure you won't have trouble cooking for a third day? I can only imagine how much work it is."

"*Nein.* I'm *gut.* I'm actually enjoying it." She thought of her idea to write a cookbook but decided that it wasn't the right time to bring up such a venture. So instead, she said, "Honestly, I usually cook dinner, anyway."

"Yes, but not for twenty people."

Everyone laughed at that, and then George moved on to address her *mamm*'s concerns. "I assume that you're open to selling items made by other women in our community."

"*Ya.* Of course. You know I have your *fraa*'s quilts, and I have all of my *doschdern* who live in the area knitting in their spare time—which is pretty limited."

"I suggest you put a call out to the community at large. I know for a fact that Donna and Meredith Bontrager have items they'd like to sell. Donna sews a lot, though they're not quilts—more like dolls, things to go on the dining table, pot holders, etcetera. Meredith has started making homemade soaps. Both are small-ticket items, but I think they'd compliment the other things you're selling."

Grace cringed at the mention of Donna and Meredith. Both had been very pointed in their disapproval of Grace, though they had never spoken to her directly. That wasn't their way. They were much more likely to talk behind her back. It was an uncharitable thought, but one she knew to be true. Still, if their items could make the tour a success, she would put aside her reservations. Her *mamm* was already nodding in agreement, so she really didn't have much choice.

"I guess we're done here, then." George stood and reached for his hat, which he plopped on his head. "You have my approval, not that you needed it, and I'll make sure that the larger tourism board is aware that you've expanded the days you're operating."

Grace was surprised when Adrian indicated he had something to say before the group dispersed.

"Some of you had reservations when we started this venture. Some of you I had to badger into giving it a try." Everyone again laughed when Adrian gave a pointed look to Grace. Even she laughed.

Had she really intentionally made a terrible casserole?

Invited bees to a picnic?

Let out Adrian's goats?

"I think we've come together as a *gut* group, and I appreciate each of you. *Danki* for taking this adventure with me, and may *Gotte* bless our endeavors as well as the people that we serve."

Murmurs of "amen" circled the group. Twenty minutes later, everyone was gone. Grace stood on the front porch with Adrian.

"Would you like to stay for dinner?"

"I'd love to, but I have a camel with several filed nails and a few unfiled nails that are probably driving her batty."

Adrian reached for Grace's hand and squeezed it, sending tiny shivers of delight down her arm and reminding her of the kisses they'd shared earlier. She wasn't a *youngie* on her first date, but oh, how her heart soared when he looked at her as he was now.

"I'd like to take you and Nicole to the Art Festival tomorrow. I saw your eyes light up when Seth mentioned it."

"*Mamm* had offered to watch Nicole, but I think she would enjoy the festival. So yes, we would love to go."

"Pick you up at ten?"

"*Ya.* Ten will be *gut.*"

The afternoon had been almost perfect. The only thing to mar it was the thought of having to work with Donna and Meredith. Later that evening, after Nicole was tucked into her bed and while her *dat* was doing a final check on the animals, Grace broached the subject with her *mamm*.

"I'm worried about including Donna and Meredith in our tour."

"Why is that, dear?"

"Certainly you're aware they aren't the most pleasant people."

"I am aware. Your *schweschder* has shared with me her problems with her in-laws many times."

Grace grimaced. The only thing worse than having to do business with those two women was to have them in your family. She would need to remember to pray for Georgia.

"What, in particular, are you worried about?" Her *mamm* was knitting a baby sweater. The needles were a blur in her hands. This time, she was using a variegated blue color that was quite beautiful.

Grace would like to have a son someday.

She'd like to have a big family.

She didn't want Nicole to be an only child. Most of the time when she thought of courting Adrian, she felt excited about the prospect, but occasionally, she fell into a rut of worrying. What if he decided he didn't want a ready-made family? What if his feelings for Grace weren't what he thought they were? What if he learned the truth about Nicole and rejected them?

She needed to tell him the truth before he heard it from someone else. She'd tried a few times, but the words had lodged in her throat.

"Grace? Would you like to share what's bothering you?"

Grace was working on the doll's dress for Nicole. She'd already finished the dress and apron for her *doschder*, but she wanted to surprise her with the doll's clothes at the same time. Each evening, she waited until Nicole was in bed to pull the project out of her sewing basket.

"Both Donna and Meredith are... *Unkind* is the nicest way to say it."

Her *mamm* raised an eyebrow, encouraging her to go on.

"I think it's because of Nicole, because of the circumstances of her birth. They judge me. Which is fine. I made my mistakes, and I don't mind paying the price for them."

"But..."

"But Nicole shouldn't have to. They shouldn't be rude to her. That's wrong, *Mamm*. That's not what the Bible teaches us."

Her *mamm* tugged on the ball of yarn and continued knitting. "The Bible says many things."

"For example?"

"It says to love your neighbors."

"*Ya.* That's what I mean. They're not loving. I wish you could see the way they treat me."

"I have seen, and it hurts my heart in the same way that seeing someone treat Nicole unkindly hurts yours. But Grace, Christ doesn't tell us to love only the neighbors who are pleasant. We're to treat everyone the way we want to be treated."

"That's not easy to do sometimes."

"You're right."

"And it makes me angry. Donna and Meredith aren't perfect. They have no right to judge me."

"You're right again, but it doesn't change a thing." Her *mamm* paused in her knitting, counted her stitches, then finished the row and stuck the needles into the ball of yarn. Scooting to the edge of the couch, she picked up the family Bible, ran her fingertips over the cover, studied it a moment and then she placed it in Grace's hands. "The answers you're looking for—they're here. But I have to warn you, I've been reading the Bible for many years and I've yet to find any promise that life will always be easy or pleasant or that people will always be kind."

"If this is a pep talk, it's terrible."

"It could be that *Gotte* has put Deborah and Meredith in our path for a reason. Perhaps we're to minister to them."

"That would be like ministering to a snake. I'm more likely to be bit for my trouble than thanked."

"We don't do it to be thanked. We do it because we're commanded to do so."

And with that, her *mamm* stood, kissed her on top of the head and headed out onto the porch to wait for her *dat*. Grace heard them out there almost every evening, usually sharing a hot cup of tea and talking over their day. Grace wanted that. She wanted someone that she could spend the last moments of each evening with as well as the first moments of each morning. She wanted someone who would care for her regardless of her past mistakes.

She honestly didn't know if Adrian was that person.

Her stomach grew queasy when she thought of confessing all to him. She would do it—soon. Not tomorrow, though. Tomorrow, she was taking Nicole to town in her new lavender dress. She scooped up her sewing things, determined to finish the doll's dress before she called it a night and equally determined to put her worries about Deborah and Meredith out of her mind. It was bad enough that she was going to have to deal with them on a weekly basis. There was no point in dragging them into her life earlier than she had to.

Because despite what her *mamm* said, she wasn't sure that they were commanded to tolerate mean people. It seemed to her that she and Nicole were both far better off avoiding them.

Chapter Eleven

Adrian's life took on a fullness and richness that he couldn't have imagined six months before. He'd found what he was missing, and he hadn't even been looking for it.

He'd found Grace and Nicole.

May gave way to June. He continued to take Grace out once a week—sometimes with the baby and sometimes without, though Nicole could hardly be called a baby now. Toward the end of June, yellow became her favorite color. She looked everywhere for it—picking yellow flowers from the roadside, falling in love with lemon slushes and wearing out her yellow crayon. Yellow bananas, baby chicks, corn, butter and daffodils were a few of her favorite things.

She was now walking like a champ and had even recently learned to run. She thought it was quite funny to make her *mamm* chase her, and though Adrian tried to look serious and disapproving, the sight of Grace chasing Nicole through his aviary brought him too much joy. He simply couldn't scold her. In that way, he might make a terrible *dat*, but he was sure he could make up for his lack of sternness another way. Perhaps it was something he could learn. He didn't expect he'd need to be firm with the little girl anytime soon, probably not until Nicole was a *youngie* and needed scolding. Fortunately, he had plenty of time before that would happen.

Grace and Nicole came to visit him nearly every day, and when they didn't, he went to their place. He kissed Grace on a regular basis now. She was still something of a mystery to him. She'd learned to relax when he reached for her hand or kissed her or complimented her, but he had the distinct impression that she was holding a part of herself back.

They spent many summer evenings walking the fields as the sun set and talking about their youth.

"You were the middle child?" She glanced up at him and smiled.

Adrian realized she could melt his heart with that smile. What wouldn't he tell her? What wouldn't he do? They were supposed to be finding out if they were right for one another—that was the purpose of a courting time—but Adrian already knew that the only woman for him was Grace Troyer.

"Can't remember?"

"Huh?"

"I asked if you were the middle child in your family." She bumped her shoulder against his.

"Oh, *ya*. I was square in the middle—five older and five younger."

"What was that like?"

"It seemed normal to me. I've heard middle children can carry a chip on their shoulder—they're not the oldest getting into trouble or the youngest causing parents to realize how quickly time passes." He plucked a weed growing by the fence line, studied it a minute and then stuck it in his mouth. "I never felt that way. To me it was more like being in a litter of pups. There was always someone to play with or drag off to see the latest animal I'd adopted."

"Even then?"

He laughed. "*Ya*. Even then. What about you? I know Georgia and Greta both live in the area."

"They attend different church districts, but they're close enough that we see them every week."

"You have other siblings, though?"

"Sure. Three married and moved away—Gloria, Gwen and Gina."

"Your *mamm* likes the letter G."

"As much as Nicole loves the color yellow."

"And you're the youngest."

"I am." She glanced at him, then looked quickly away.

"Something you want to add to that?"

"Only that being the youngest, well... Sometimes it means you make mistakes that others didn't. My *schweschdern* were already married and out of the house by the time I was a *youngie*."

"I'm sure you did the best you could."

She studied him then, as if to see whether he really meant it. Finally, she said, "I hope you always believe that."

"Of course I do... I will."

They'd been to dinner at both Greta's and Georgia's. Adrian thought both of Grace's *schweschdern* approved of their courting. At least they were polite to him, and their *kinner* were full of questions about his animals.

He and Grace came to know one another's childhood through those long walks. But a wall seemed to appear between them whenever they spoke of their teen-age years. Adrian didn't mind admitting the times he'd stepped outside their *Ordnung.* Once when he was four-teen, he'd tried to drive a car and ended up steering it into a ditch. Another time, he thought it was when he was sixteen but really couldn't remember, he'd tried smoking and ended up coughing for an hour.

Grace listened attentively to his stories, but she didn't share any details about her own *rumspringa.*

Adrian thought the whole idea of *rumspringa* had been overemphasized. Without fail, every single tour group asked him about the practice. Many of them had read about it in books or seen it depicted in television shows. He had no idea how accurate those things were. He could speak only to his own experience and that of his siblings. When he explained that *rumspringa* was a time for teens to try the *Englisch* world, to experience what they would vow to give up when they joined the church, the folks in the tour group invariably look baffled.

"So your parents approve of your smoking and drink-ing?"

"*Nein.* It's not like that. It's more that they want us to experience those things that we're curious about be-fore we give them up. Things like going to a movie in town or driving a car—or yes, even smoking a ciga-rette. They'd never give us money for cigarettes and if you know how much they cost…" At this point, several *Englischers* would always nod their understanding. "So you understand that it's not like an Amish teen is going to run to town and buy a carton of smokes. There's no way he or she could afford it!"

He'd go on to explain that many of the things that happened during *rumspringa* were normal things for teens, but for Amish, it was more like poking a toe into the *Englisch* world.

"What if a teenager decides they like it? Decides they enjoy movies at the cinema and cell phones?"

"I can't speak for everyone, but in my extended family, you're usually shipped off to a Mennonite *aenti* or *onkel* at that point. Mennonites are very much like Amish but somewhat less strict. So they live there awhile before they make a decision. Of course they can come back anytime they want."

"No shunning?"

"Shunnings are exceedingly rare these days, and I don't mind admitting I'm glad. As our bishop once said, he'd never tell us we can't see or speak with a family member. *Gotte* leads each person in a different way."

"Your bishop sounds pretty progressive."

Adrian had shrugged and turned the topic to his animals. But here and now, speaking with Grace, he thought about those conversations again. Even when they occurred during the meal they fed the tourists, Grace didn't chime in.

She didn't speak of *rumspringa* publicly or privately.

Instead, she'd change the subject or ask him another question.

He hoped that the closer they became, the more comfortable she would feel sharing. But by July, he was beginning to suspect that might not ever happen. Which was okay with him. He loved Grace regardless of what silly antics she'd done during her *rumspringa*. After all, how bad could it be? She was in the new-member class. She was joining the church.

Then the two letters arrived. One a day after the other. The first was penned in feminine handwriting and contained a single line. "Ask Grace about Nicole's father."

There was no signature or return address. He'd tossed the letter onto his junk-mail pile, which threatened to topple off the kitchen counter, and given it little thought.

Then the second letter arrived. It was rather more pointed. "You should know why Grace moved to Ohio before you decide to marry her."

That was signed "a friend." Adrian somehow doubted that whoever had penned it was a friend. More than likely, it was someone who was sticking their nose where it didn't belong.

Adrian picked up the stack of junk mail including both letters, which were definitely junk, and carried them out to the old metal barrel where he burned trash. Throwing a match into the can and watching the paper flame, he frowned.

Trash.

That was what those letters were. They were rubbish. He didn't know what motivated people to be nosy. He didn't know why sometimes people—even *gut* people—treated one another poorly. But he did understand it was one of the reasons he was more comfortable with animals.

Take Millie the blind albino donkey he'd recently acquired. Triangle would start barking anytime Millie ended up somewhere she shouldn't be. Even Kendrick treated the donkey kindly—blocking the door to the aviary when Adrian inadvertently left it open. He didn't have to worry about the birds flying out and not returning. They knew where the feeding stations were. He liked leaving the door open so the birds could enjoy the great outdoors.

But a blind donkey in his aviary could create a real mess. Millie might even manage to get hurt. But she never went in, because Kendrick always blocked the way. He would find them in something of a standoff, with Millie trying to push her way in and Kendrick moving left, then right, then left again to impede her progress.

Whenever that happened, Adrian would relocate Millie to her pasture and give Kendrick an extra treat.

Animals seemed to display the very characteristics that were missing in people. Perhaps they were just looking out for their own unusual herd, but shouldn't people do the same? Shouldn't they lift one another up instead of bringing each other down?

Adrian struggled with these questions as he attempted to give Grace the time and space she needed.

The evening after he'd received—and burned—the second letter, he'd gone to see Grace as was his custom when she hadn't stopped by during the day. It was mid-July, and they'd been properly courting more than two months.

He had absolutely no intention of bringing up the letters, but he was irritated by them. As he and Grace sat on the back porch, watching Nicole toddle around her swing set, some of that irritation must have leaked out.

"What's bugging you?" Grace asked.

"Nothing." Then deciding that it was best to be as honest as possible, he added, "Why can't people just do what's right?"

Grace took her eyes off Nicole to study him. "What do you mean? What people? And how are you sure what's right?"

"Just regular people."

"Not very specific."

"Let's say—hypothetically—Plain people."

"Okay. And these Plain people did something wrong?"

"*Ya.* They did." It may have come out more forcefully than he intended, but this was Grace's business they were poking around in. How dare they?

"Maybe they didn't know it was wrong."

"Anyone would."

"Maybe they couldn't help themselves."

"Of course they could help themselves. It's just easier to do the wrong thing, to give in to the wrong impulse. It's easier to pretend you're not Plain and to have a foot in both worlds. That's not how we live, though. That's not how we're supposed to live. We're supposed to be different."

"Oh, come on, Adrian. You're not that uncharitable."

"I'm serious. Just do the right thing."

"Oh, it's that simple, is it? Like when you know that you can't afford another animal, but you adopt a blind donkey anyway?"

"Millie's adjusting quite well…and it's not like that at all. I'm talking about a moral choice where someone intentionally chooses wrong. It could hurt people, and they should be more responsible."

Grace stood up, arms crossed, a tiny frown forming between her eyes. He'd seen that look a few times. Bad things usually followed, but did he pay any heed to that warning in his head? *Nein.* He did not.

"You are not perfect, Adrian Schrock."

"I never said I was."

"Maybe you haven't been in an uncomfortable position, where choosing the wrong thing doesn't seem like a choice at all."

"I have no idea what that means."

"Perhaps you shouldn't be judging people."

"Who put a bee under your *kapp* today?"

Grace's eyes widened. "I do not have a bee under my *kapp*, and I'll thank you not to make fun of me."

"I wasn't making fun, Grace. I was only venting my feelings, is all. Can't a man do that with his girlfriend?"

"He can, but then he risks hearing the other side of an argument—something you don't appear prepared to do."

Adrian felt his pulse accelerate and his body tense. He thought there might be smoke coming out of his ears. He was protecting her, but he couldn't tell Grace that unless he wanted to confess all about the letters. And what good would that do? Now she was mad at him. Some days, women made no sense at all to him. He stood and slapped the hat he'd been holding back on his head.

"Guess I should be going home."

"Fine. Go home."

"You don't seem in the mood for visiting."

"No doubt your animals are better company than I am."

"When you're acting like this… *Ya*, they are."

Which caused Grace's face to turn a charming pink. She opened her mouth, raised her finger to shake it at him and then Nicole let out a scream that split the summer evening and caused all other concerns to fall away.

Grace was about to set Adrian straight. How could he think that he always knew what was right? He was no better than Deborah and Meredith, who she'd had about enough of. Their under-the-breath comments and superior looks had just about pushed her to the edge of her patience. Adrian wasn't helping things, and it wasn't her fault that he had picked this evening of all evenings to start an ethical debate.

But when she opened her mouth to tell him exactly how wrong he was, Nicole's scream stopped her short.

Where was Nicole?

Grace turned, saw her standing at the base of the yellow slide, covered in mud. How had she...?

There hadn't been rain in over a week.

There wasn't any mud.

And then she was sprinting toward her *doschder*. She scooped her up and slapped at the ants that had covered her arms and legs.

Adrian ran for the water hose and proceeded to squirt the ants off her, revealing dozens of large red welts. Dropping the hose, he said, "I'll get your *dat*'s buggy."

He dashed around the house as her *mamm* came outside to see what was wrong. By the time they'd wrapped Nicole's arms and legs in wet towels, then bundled her up in a summer blanket, Adrian had brought the horse and buggy around.

Grace's *mamm* pushed her purse into her hands. "Go. Straight to the hospital. We'll bring Adrian's buggy and be right behind you."

Adrian set their mare into a gallop.

"How is she?" Adrian didn't take his eyes off the road.

"I don't know. Nicole, honey. Look at me."

"Is she breathing okay?"

"I think she is."

But in fact, Nicole seemed to be having trouble pulling in a good breath. Was she having an allergic reaction to the ant bites? Or was she breathless from her sobbing? She refused to be consoled. The ride to the hospital seemed to take hours and also seemed to happen instantly. One minute, Grace was standing in the back-yard with her baby girl, and the next, they were rushing through the doors of the emergency room.

The next hour was a blur.

She filled out a clipboard full of forms, though she couldn't have told anyone what she wrote on them.

A nurse ushered her through a pair of double doors. She glanced back just once and saw Adrian standing in the middle of the room, his hat in his hands and a lost expression on his face. She wanted to run to him, to feel his arms around her and to apologize for flying off at him. She didn't do any of those things. Instead, she carried Nicole into their assigned room and placed her on the bed.

The nurse asked more questions.

A doctor arrived and examined Nicole. "She's having some difficulty breathing. This happens occasionally with allergic reactions. We'll give her Benadryl through an IV drip. She'll be right as rain in no time."

The nurses were good. They'd dealt with children many times through many different types of situations. One distracted Nicole with a puppet while another started the IV. The poke of the needle brought more cries from her *doschder*, but then she looked back at the puppet and seemed to forget the ouchie on her arm. The nurse placed a wrap around her arm—perhaps so Nicole wouldn't attempt to mess with the IV. The wrap was decorated with bright flowers, and Nicole touched the yellow ones—alternately crying, hiccupping or calling out, "Yellow, *Mamm*. Yellow."

Grace had no idea how much time had passed when she heard a light tap on the door and looked up to see her mother standing there.

And that was when the tears started.

"It happened so fast. I should have been watching her more closely."

Nicole was curled on her side, now fast asleep. Grace's *mamm* came in and sat down beside her, placing one hand on top of Grace's hand and the other on her cheek. "I'm sorry, Grace. This is what being a mother is about. You can't watch them all the time, and you can't protect them from everything that will hurt them."

"Then it's too hard. Being a *mamm* is too hard. I would rather have all of those ant bites—double the number, even—on me."

"Of course you would, but we don't always have that choice. You did the right thing. You reacted quickly and kept your head on straight."

Grace didn't answer that. Her *mamm* patted her arm, waited a few minutes and finally said, "Do you remember the time that you and Georgia disturbed that beehive and came running inside, screaming as if a pack of wolves was chasing you?"

"I was five."

"You were. Georgia was seven. I blamed myself for that little incident. If only I'd been watching you more closely, if only I'd kept you inside, if only…"

"One stung me on the eyelid." Grace reached up and brushed a finger along the small scar. She hadn't thought of that incident in years. The pain had been sharp and her eye had swollen instantly. She'd feared she would never be able to see again.

"Your eye swelled completely shut. I rushed you to the hospital that day, just like you and Adrian rushed Nicole here tonight."

"And what did the doctors do?"

"They gave you Benadryl in an IV and put a compress

on your eye. Georgia had bites on her neck. She walked around for a week with her hands wrapped around her neck if she was outside. I felt like a terrible *mamm*."

"You were a *gut mamm*. You always were."

"*Nein.* I had my days where I was less than that, but I think you girls know how much I love you. That's the true test. Isn't it?"

The doctor walked in and checked Nicole's breathing. After he made a notation on his tablet, he looked at them and smiled. "She's responding well to the Benadryl. We'll want to see her awake and eating before we let her go home."

"So she can go tonight?"

"Sure. She should be home by bedtime."

After the doctor left, her *mamm* pulled out some knitting—this time, it looked she was making a sweater of light yellow wool.

"For Nicole?"

"Of course."

"But you should be knitting for the *Englisch* tourists."

"If I'm ever too busy to knit for my own *grandkinner*, then I'm too busy."

Grace watched her for a few minutes, then said, "I don't know how you focus."

Her *mamm* smiled, the needles and yarn a blur in her hands. She finished a row, checked her marker, then dropped the knitting back into her bag. "I'll tell you a secret. The reason I love to knit is that it's predictable. Dependable. If I follow the pattern carefully, if I knit when I should knit and purl when I should purl, if I count my stitches, then the thing I'm making turns out correctly every time."

"That does not happen when I knit," Grace admitted,

but then she rarely remembered to count her stitches, and she often purled in the wrong place.

"It's comforting to me, for sure and certain." Her *mamm* stared at Nicole for a moment, then looked back at Grace, a smile playing on her lips. "Life isn't predictable in that way. It never has been. Knitting helps me to feel grounded. It helps the crazy days feel…manageable."

Her *mamm* stood, walked over to Nicole and kissed her on the top of the head. She paused when she reached the door and looked back. "Your *dat* and Adrian would like to come in."

"*Ya*, of course."

Her *dat* stayed less than five minutes. It was as if he needed to see for himself that Nicole was fine, and then he was content to leave the details of her care to Grace.

"Would you like us to wait around until the doctor is ready to dismiss her?"

Grace glanced up at Adrian, and maybe for the first time, she fully realized how much he cared about her and Nicole, because the expression on his face told her that he needed and wanted to be the one to take them home.

"*Nein*, *dat*. *Danki*, though. Adrian will bring us home."

Her *dat* nodded, as if that was what he'd expected her to say.

Which left Grace alone in the room with Adrian and her sleeping child. Adrian had purchased a get-well card from the hospital gift shop. The card sported a teddy bear carrying a large bouquet of balloons. "It was the only thing I could find with the color yellow." He placed the card on the little stand holding Nicole's cup and pitcher of water. Then he stepped closer to the bed, bent down and kissed Nicole on the head.

When he met Grace's gaze, she moved her purse off the chair beside hers and motioned toward it. He sat down heavily, with a sigh that seemed to come from the center of his bones.

"I've never been so scared."

"Me, too."

"You acted quickly, Grace. You were—you were amazing."

"You're the one who thought of the water hose." She glanced down at her apron, which had been quite wet but was finally dry. Rubbing her palm over a water stain, she said, *"Danki."*

"For what?"

"Bringing us here. You didn't have to do that. She's not…" Her lips trembled and she pulled the bottom one in, drew a deep breath and pushed forward. "She's not yours, but you reacted as if she was."

He claimed her hand. Adrian liked holding hands, and Grace found great comfort in his touch—in that connection between them.

"Grace, I care about you and Nicole. Maybe more than you know."

She nodded and rested her head against his shoulder. She was suddenly quite exhausted. The clock on the wall assured her it was only eight in the evening, but it felt much later. "I'm sorry," she whispered.

"For what?"

"Arguing with you. Flying off the handle. Losing my patience. Take your pick."

He leaned away, holding her at arm's length. "What? You're not perfect?"

"I most certainly am not."

Adrian pulled her back against his side. "Duly noted."

Then he added, "In case you're wondering, I'm not perfect, either."

"Two imperfect people." Grace offered a fake shudder.

"We'll push our way through whatever comes our way."

"Like ant bites."

"Yup."

"And silly arguments."

"Those, too."

They were silent for a moment, but the earlier fight still weighed on her. It all seemed so trivial now. "As you've probably noticed, there are some subjects that are a bit touchy for me."

"Uh-huh."

"Like *rumspringa* and mistakes and not being perfect."

He didn't respond. He simply waited. She loved that about him—his willingness to wait and let her gather her thoughts."

"I made mistakes, Adrian. During my *rumspringa*. There are things…things that you don't know about me." She was too tired to cry. Too tired to protect her secrets.

He didn't move away.

He didn't question her.

Instead, he kissed her on top of the head—it seemed everyone was kissing her head—and whispered, "I love you, Grace."

Then tears did sting her eyes. She closed them, trying to find just the right words to lay out her past. Now was as good a time as any. In fact, it was the perfect time. They were alone. It was quiet. Adrian didn't need to dash off and care for an animal.

But the day's emotional highs and lows had been

too much. The adrenaline that had propelled her across the yard to rescue Nicole was gone. She was left with a deep-seated tiredness. Her thoughts circled round and round—Nicole crying, thinking she was covered in mud, seeing ants, Nicole's face looking up in confusion, then the piercing cry. Running toward her. Adrian suddenly at her side with water. The mad dash to town. The doctors and nurses and the yellow get-well card.

Her head nodded and she nearly allowed herself to sleep. She tried to remember what they were talking about. *Rumspringa.* She needed to tell Adrian about her past. She rubbed both hands over her face, stood and fetched a cup of water, then sat down beside him. Still, he waited.

"I need to tell you something."

"Okay."

But it wasn't meant to be, apparently, because for the second time that night, Nicole interrupted them. This time, she was calling for her *mamm* and exclaiming over the "yellow boons" and demanding something to eat because she was hungry.

The nurse bustled into the room carrying a tray with Jell-O and a small box of juice.

The chance to confess all to Adrian slipped away, but Grace would do so. Maybe not in the next hour, maybe not even that night, but she would tell him. Because he mattered, and she didn't want anything to loom between them.

She knew, with complete certainty, that the only way to move forward was to face her past.

Chapter Twelve

The trip to the hospital changed Adrian. He'd understood that he cared for both Grace and Nicole before that mad-dash ride into town. He'd realized he was happier and more at peace when he was around them. But now he accepted that they had changed his life in some fundamental way.

When he woke in the morning, his first thought was of them.

As he worked, he'd toss around ideas of various ways to brighten their day.

When he went to bed at night, they were the last images on his mind.

His life wasn't about himself anymore or even about his animals—though the zoo brought meaning and purpose to his daily work. He loved sharing *Gotte*'s creatures with folks who attended the tours. But they weren't the reason he'd been placed on this world. He was there to love and care for and cherish Grace and Nicole.

Within twenty-four hours of the ant attack, Nicole was back to her old self—toddling around, delighting over any yellow item and proudly showing off her boo-

boos. Nicole was the same sweet, precocious child she'd always been.

But Adrian was forever changed, and it seemed that Grace was, as well. There was a softness about her now, as if the wall that had existed between them had finally been breached. Perhaps that was the purpose of hard times. Maybe they brought two people together in ways that a dozen afternoon picnics could not.

The extra tours and additional animals—he'd picked up an injured owl, several axis deer and a miniature pig—claimed much of his attention. He saw Grace every day, but sometimes it was for only a few minutes. He vowed to change that, and soon.

It was time to ask Grace to be his *fraa*. It was past time. Why hadn't he asked six weeks ago? But he'd never asked a woman to marry him. He wasn't exactly sure how it was done. Where would be the best place to ask her, or did that even matter? What was the best way to explain how much she meant to him?

He wasn't *Englisch*. He couldn't simply drive into town, stop at the local jewelry store and buy a diamond ring large enough to represent his love. Amish didn't wear jewelry. But picking a bouquet of wildflowers seemed somewhat inadequate.

He needed someone else's opinion, someone he trusted. George had been helpful, but he wasn't sure how much George understood women. What he needed was a woman's perspective. So five days after the hospital trip, Adrian hitched up his buggy and went to see his *schweschder*, Beth. She was only three years older, and she'd always seemed to understand him in a way that the rest of the family didn't. She'd even understood his need to open an exotic-animal farm. Beth was the one who had told his parents, "*Gotte* put this dream in Adrian's heart. Let Adrian see if he can make a living from it."

He'd sought her advice many times that first year. Now Adrian needed to talk to someone about Grace. He needed to decide if his next step was the right one. He didn't want to go too slow...or too fast.

"Surprised to see you in the middle of the day." Beth was out behind the house hanging laundry on the line.

His six nieces and nephews were scattered about the place. The oldest was five and there were two sets of twins. He didn't know how she handled them all, but everyone seemed happy and healthy. Several came running to hug his legs, or ask if he'd brought any of his animals with him, or demand that he come and see something.

"*Ya, ya.* But let me talk to your *mamm* first."

Beth raised an eyebrow, then motioned to the back porch. The temperature was average for July but still quite hot. She fetched two glasses of iced tea.

"Ice? You're getting all *Englisch* on me."

"Yes, well—the new propane refrigerator we bought has a larger freezer area. I claimed a corner for ice trays. Take a sip. You'll see. It's very cooling."

He drank half the glass in one gulp. "Hits the spot, for sure and certain." Then he pulled off his hat and wiped his brow.

"So what's this thing you need to talk about?"

Beth was good about that. She never wasted time beating around the bush.

"I want to ask Grace to marry me."

"I see."

"I love her."

"Do you now?"

"And I love Nicole. I want them to be my family. I

want *kinner* and a home and a *fraa* to share my days, to share my life with."

"Well. That's quite a speech. I believe I need some oatmeal bars to help me digest this news."

She scooped up a child and dropped her in Adrian's lap. Another was yawning and rubbing his eyes, so she carried him inside. "Give me a minute. I'm putting this one down for a nap."

He heard a sleepy "But I'm not tired, *Mamm*" as they walked away.

She returned for the *boppli* that Adrian was holding— the boy had been named Aidan because Beth had thought the infant looked like his *onkel*.

"This one needs to go down, too," she cooed as she reached for the child.

When she returned, she was carrying a plate of oatmeal bars, which the remaining children rushed to consume.

"One each, and I set cups of water on the kitchen table. Take them inside."

Finally, she turned her attention back to Adrian. "I'm happy for you, *bruder*. I really am."

"But?"

"I didn't say *but*."

"And yet I heard one nonetheless."

She didn't answer right away, which was strange for Beth. Usually she knew what she wanted to say and had no problem saying it. Her youngest, who was close to Nicole's age, crawled up into her lap, and she set to rocking the child.

"Grace and Nicole will be a *gut* addition to our family."

"I agree."

"Have you told Mamm and Dat?"

"*Nein.* I haven't even asked Grace yet."

"But you think she'll say yes."

"I hope and pray she will."

Beth nodded as if he'd confirmed everything she'd been thinking. "How much do you and Grace talk?"

"We talk every day."

"*Nein*. I mean…" She waved a hand back toward the kitchen, where they could just make out the sound of her three oldest children talking. "Sometimes it's hard to have a real conversation with *bopplin* around."

Adrian thought about the discussion he'd had with Grace in the hospital. It had seemed she was about to tell him something important, then Nicole had awakened and they'd shifted their attention to her.

"We're both pretty busy," he admitted.

"Daniel and I try to spend a half hour or more on the back porch each evening, no matter how tired we are. We need that time to speak to one another without interruptions."

"Okay."

"Make time to speak with Grace. That would be my advice."

"Okay." This time, he said it more slowly. He wasn't really sure what the big deal was, but he trusted that if Beth said it was important, then it was.

He stood and stretched, then walked down the porch steps.

His nephew Joshua dashed past him before turning around and walking backward. "Come on, Onkel Adrian. You said you'd come take a look."

"Guess I'll go see what that's about."

"Probably a nest he spied in one of the maple trees. Your nephew has your fascination with animals."

"*Gut* to hear." He walked toward Joshua, who had run

to the tree and was now lying under it, staring up into its branches, but Beth called him back.

"When you talk to Grace, try to be open."

"Open?"

"Don't be so didactic."

"Didactic?"

"Stop repeating what I say. You know what the word means."

"I'm not didactic."

"You tend toward declarative statements."

"What are you talking about?"

"Don't end every comment or thought with an exclamation point. Try a few question marks." She readjusted the sleeping toddler in her arms. "Sometimes what you think is right isn't right every time in every way."

"That makes no sense!"

"See? A declarative statement. It's one of your faults."

Adrian jerked off his hat and slapped it against his leg. He did not speak in declarative statements. Not all the time anyway.

She smiled at him. "How else could you say what you just said—'that makes no sense'?"

"Um…"

"Try something like 'That doesn't really make sense to me. Could you explain what you mean?'"

Adrian rolled his eyes. "It's not like that between me and Grace. We understand each other."

"Right."

But twenty minutes later, as he was driving back toward his place, he remembered the argument they'd had over *rumspringa* and choosing right from wrong. Had he been didactic then?

He didn't think so.

But maybe…

Well, if he had been, he wouldn't be anymore. He loved Grace, and he was going to tell her so and ask her to marry him. And then he'd listen, and he wouldn't judge.

Perhaps he should make a list of pointers for how to go about having a conversation with her. Just when he thought he'd conquered this courting thing, just when he was feeling confident around Grace, his *schweschder* had to go and throw a stick in his buggy wheel.

Unfortunately, the more he thought about it, the more convinced he became that possibly she had a point.

He could always count on Beth to be honest with him. The smart thing would be to follow her advice.

He'd reclaimed his good mood by the time he pulled into his lane. He could do this. And hopefully within the next few nights, he'd find time to speak with Grace alone. Then they could begin their life together.

Two days later, Grace received word that Adrian's *dat* had suffered a heart attack.

"They say it was a small one." Beth had stopped by on her way home from the hospital. "They say it's *gut* we made it to the hospital so quickly."

"It's hard to think of a heart attack as *gut* in any way."

"True, but his cardiologist says very little of the heart muscle was damaged. They put stents in two other arteries and are starting him on blood thinners and statins to lower his cholesterol."

"So, will he be okay?"

"Oh, *ya*. The doctor says he might be plowing the fields again by fall, but he needs to take it easy—stop working ten-hour days."

"Will he do that?"

Beth shrugged. "My *mamm* can be pretty bossy if she needs to be. If the doctor says to shorten his work-day, Mamm will see that he cuts back on the hours he spends in the fields."

Grace thought of her own father. He seemed so healthy. It was hard to conceive that her parents could grow old and develop health problems, though most people did. She had a sudden urge to find them and give them both a big hug.

"Adrian asked me to stop and bring you up-to-date. He's sorry he hasn't been by to visit."

"Oh!" Grace felt her face blush.

Beth's smile grew until her eyes squinted.

Grace felt ridiculous. Why couldn't she control the way her body reacted when someone mentioned Adrian's name? She wasn't a *youngie* anymore. She swiped at hair that had escaped from her *kapp*. "It's no problem. He needs to be there for his family. We understand."

Beth lowered her voice and leaned out the window. "He came to see me about you."

"What?" Grace squeaked. Forcing her voice lower, she asked, "Um…what do you mean?"

"Just needed someone to talk to, I guess. He's been bouncing his feelings and ideas off me for years."

"Oh."

"He cares about you, Grace."

"I see. We…that is I…actually Nicole and I and even my parents, we care about him, too."

Beth picked up the reins and released the brake on the buggy. "Don't worry if you don't see him for a few days."

"Okay."

"Or weeks."

"Weeks?"

"He's going to have his hands full, taking care of those animals on his place while at the same time helping at my parents' until our *dat* gets back on his feet."

"Of course."

"But he's thinking about you both, and he'll be by when he can. That was his exact message." She offered a little wave, then called out to the mare.

Grace watched Adrian's *schweschder* disappear down the lane.

He'd talked to Beth about her?

He was thinking of her?

And he'd stop by when he could?

It wasn't the way she'd envisioned the next few weeks going, but then life often threw surprises out in the middle of the road. Surely she could handle a few weeks of not seeing him.

She kept herself busy tending their vegetable garden and cooking for the tour groups. Seth took over guiding guests through Adrian's farm. Grace sewed more clothes for Nicole, who was growing faster than the green bean vines in the garden. Grace also attended the last of her baptism classes. The final lesson covered excommunication and separation from the church. The topic terrified her. She loved and valued her church. She didn't want to be separated from it.

Bishop Luke explained that this was a last resort.

That they sought to council wayward members first.

That it didn't apply to sins they'd committed before they'd become members.

That no one was perfect.

Still, the entire topic caused a rock to form in Grace's belly. She loved her community, and she always wanted to remain a part of it. Even people like Donna and Meredith were important members. They had a terrible attitude, but the items they sold to the tour groups were quite popular. Perhaps something in their past caused their bitterness. Maybe there was a reason for their distrust of others.

Grace didn't know, but she did know that she'd rather be a part of their church community than not be a part of it.

Perhaps more important, she felt genuine regret that she'd stepped outside *Gotte*'s plan for her life. She loved Nicole. She was grateful for Nicole. Perhaps her *doschder* was *Gotte*'s way of bringing her back into the fold. If she hadn't become pregnant, she might have stayed on that wayward path much longer. Her *doschder* had brought her home to her family, to her church and to Adrian.

Adrian.

She missed him more than she would have thought possible.

Georgia stopped over to drop off a few items she'd knitted. She'd left her children at home with her mother-in-law, and Nicole was down for a nap. It was a good time for the two sisters to talk.

"How are things going with Adrian?"

"*Gut.* I've hardly seen him since his *dat*'s heart attack."

"Will stopped over yesterday to help in the fields. He said that Adrian's *dat* looks much better—his color is healthy and his energy is returning."

"I didn't realize how much I looked forward to Adrian's visits."

They were pulling laundry off the line, folding it and placing it in large wicker baskets. As Grace pulled off a sheet, Georgia unpinned the other end. They folded it in half, then Georgia walked toward her and matched the ends together.

"I should have told him." Grace's words were soft but certain. She'd missed an important opportunity at the hospital. Let that be a lesson to her—do the important thing when you can. Don't put it off. Don't think you'll have time tomorrow. "I wish I had talked to him already."

"About?"

"Nicole…and Kolby."

"So, tell him."

"It's harder now. It feels like…sort of like I've been lying to him all this time."

"I guess you have and you haven't. They say a lie of omission is the same as any other lie."

"Thanks. That's helpful."

"Just tell him. What's the worst that could happen?"

They finished folding the sheet, and Grace placed it in the basket.

"He could decide he doesn't want to be with a woman like me."

"A woman like you?"

"One who's made a mistake." There, she'd said it! Why was it so hard to talk about such things?

Georgia finished folding a towel, then sat down in one of the lawn chairs and patted the one next to her. Grace joined her, suddenly too tired to unpin another piece of laundry. She still had those days, where she felt fine one minute and exhausted the next. Maybe she did have the baby blues, or maybe holding such a big secret in her heart was taking its toll.

"You want to tell Adrian the truth?"

"I do. I want to tell everyone. I want everyone to know that Nicole is my *doschder*."

"Okay. My advice is to start with Adrian. He deserves to hear it first."

"And if he rejects me?"

"Grace, if he rejects you, then he's not the man *Gotte* intended for you to spend your life with. Better to know now how he responds, before your feelings grow even more." She reached forward and brushed Grace's *kapp* string to the back. "There will always be some people who judge."

"Like Deborah and Meredith."

"Yes. Exactly. We're not responsible for those people or their reactions."

"But what does that mean?"

"It means you should live your life the way you think you're supposed to live it, and stop worrying about other people."

"Right."

"Talk to Adrian."

"I will."

"Soon."

"Okay."

Grace felt immeasurably better making that promise to Georgia. No more procrastinating. No more acting like a child. It was time to move forward, hopefully with Adrian, but even if it meant doing so without him, she needed to move forward. Being stuck was worse than having to move in a different direction.

She was ready.

Then Adrian's *dat* had a slight setback. He returned to the hospital, though they released him after three days. He'd tried to do too much too fast. Adrian would be needed there at the family farm a little longer.

Two weeks passed, then three. August arrived and the day of her baptism drew nearer.

Then the rains began.

Chapter Thirteen

Goshen, Indiana, received an average of four inches of rain each month during the summer. Grace knew this, because her *dat*—like most farmers—found the topic of weather and rain and averages to be fascinating. Her *dat* was quite happy when they received five days straight of solid rain.

"*Gut* for the crops," he reminded her when she stood by the window, frowning out at the clouds.

"Yes, but not so *gut* for little girls." Grace thought that she'd never view rain the same again after having a cooped-up eighteen-month-old to contend with.

Grace had woke on Friday morning to the sound of more rain hitting the windowpanes. "Great," she murmured, and pulled the quilt up to her chin. But soon she heard her *mamm* downstairs in the kitchen, and then Nicole called out from her room across the hall. It was time to face another day trapped in this house.

Which meant facing another day when she probably wouldn't see Adrian. No doubt this rain was causing a lot of havoc with his exotic animals. As far as she knew, he'd started work on an ark.

They had breakfast, Grace cleaned the house a bit, then she and her *mamm* pulled out their needlework, but Grace couldn't concentrate. She was attempting a sweater in yellow for Nicole, but something had gone terribly wrong with the sleeves. She sighed and set about pulling out the last few rows she'd knitted.

They ate lunch.

Knitted some more.

She read a few picture books to Nicole.

The rain finally slowed to a soft drip, certainly less than the downpour they'd endured all morning. No doubt another round of heavy rain was coming. Though the clock read two in the afternoon, it seemed more like dusk outside. Grace had pulled the pillows off her bed and scattered them on top of a blanket in the kitchen in front of the large window. Nicole sat there like a queen on her throne, playing with her baby doll and talking to her in a whisper.

"You should go and check on him." Her *mamm* pushed a cup of coffee into her hands. "After you drink this. You look as if you could use a little caffeine."

Grace sipped the coffee, which was delicious. Unfortunately, it did nothing to mitigate the restlessness coursing through her veins.

"This storm system has to move on eventually."

"Indeed. But until then, it helps to get out whenever it eases up, as it has now."

"You want me to walk over to Adrian's...in this weather?"

"It's plenty warm enough. Wear my rain boots and a light sweater. Oh, and take the umbrella." She hesitated, then added, "Trust me, you'll feel better if you talk to him. You haven't seen him since he finished up working his *dat*'s fields."

Grace looked fully at her *mamm* then, and in that moment, she knew that her *mamm* had guessed her feelings for Adrian. She'd never been good at hiding such things.

Now her *mamm* squeezed her hand and said, "Baby girl is about to go down for a nap."

Sure enough, Nicole was now lying on the blanket, fingers stuck in her mouth, baby doll clutched close to her side.

"You won't even need to move her."

"Exactly. Now go, and tell Adrian to come over here for dinner. He probably hasn't had a good meal since this rain started five days ago."

By the time Grace had fetched a sweater—taking ten minutes to decide between the blue or dark green, and finally opting for the blue, hoping it helped her complexion to look less pale—found an umbrella and donned her *mamm*'s rain boots, Nicole was fast asleep.

Her *mamm* had poured coffee into a thermos. Now she handed it to Nicole along with a lunch pail. "Fresh peanut butter bars in there." Stepping closer, she put a hand on each side of Grace's face and kissed her forehead, then nudged her toward the door.

But she called her back before she stepped outside.

"Do you remember the emergency signal?"

"*Ya.* Um…find a window and put two candles in it."

"One means all is right."

"Two means send help."

"Candles or lanterns. I suspect that Adrian is fine. No doubt he's in that old barn with his animals, but in case there's a problem, we can see the barn from here. So if you need us, put two lights in the window and I'll send your *dat* right over."

Which pretty much summed up her *mamm*'s attitude

toward life. Get on out there. Do what you need or simply want to do. But have a plan ready if things take a turn for the worse.

Grace hurried down the porch steps and to the lane, dodging giant puddles and small rivulets that threatened to turn into streams. It was actually a bit lighter outside than she had thought, though as she looked to the west, she saw darker clouds and knew they were about to get slammed again. She stopped, looked back toward the house and wondered if she should abandon this fool's errand.

But her *mamm* was right. They should check on Adrian.

Plus, Nicole was fine. She needed to stop using her *doschder* as an excuse for avoiding the uncomfortable. She turned and continued toward the main road, made a right, then skirted more puddles as she walked to the lane that led into Adrian's property. No one was out on the road. No cars. No buggies. People were buttoned-down for the storm, and they had been for the entire week now.

Her heartbeat quickened at the thought of seeing Adrian. Did he feel the same way that she did? When had she fallen in love with him? When had she lowered her defenses enough to begin caring for someone?

Perhaps it had been when she'd let the goats out and he hadn't become angry.

Maybe it had happened after Nicole's ear infection, when she'd visited his place and they'd taken that walk and he'd first held her hand. Or perhaps it had been the first time he'd kissed her, when they'd been standing in Cinnamon's pen. She smiled to herself at that memory.

She could see his barn now, but none of the animals came to greet her. In fact, it was eerily deserted, though as she passed the aviary she did hear birdsong.

But where was Adrian?

Where were his animals?

She hadn't realized that his property was lower than theirs. The water here was much deeper, and she was glad she'd worn the rain boots. The barn was on a bit of a hill, and it took her twice as long as usual to even reach it. Turning to look back the way she'd come, she realized that Adrian's place resembled several ponds more than anything else.

She nearly slipped in the mud twice as she made her way up to the main doors. She thought of her *mamm*'s admonition about the emergency signal. Glancing back toward their place, she saw the single battery-operated lantern in the window. Her *mamm* must have placed it there after she left.

She turned back toward the barn and pulled in a deep, cleansing breath. The walk had helped to clear her head. She knew what she needed to do. She needed to tell Adrian how she felt. She needed to find out whether he felt the same. Not knowing was making her crazy. So she murmured a prayer for courage, then raised her hand and knocked on the door, but no one answered. Thinking he couldn't hear her, she pounded on it. Finally, she pushed open the door to the main section of the barn, and when she peered inside she didn't know whether to laugh or run for help.

Cinnamon stood in the main portion of the barn, and the camel seemed twice as big as normal, twice as big as when she was outside in her fenced area. She turned her large head toward Grace, then back toward the bucket of feed.

Kendrick was on the other side of the room, and for once, he seemed subdued. Perhaps the camel had finally settled their score, or maybe there was nowhere for him to run, so he'd decided to behave himself.

Those two animals looked so incongruous together that Grace felt laughter bubble up inside. They pretty much represented Adrian and what he was trying to do here—bring together every strange and diverse animal that needed a home and teach them to coexist.

Grace heard Triangle's bark, and she followed the sound down the north side of the barn, past the stall holding Adrian's buggy horse, who seemed to be sleeping, then back outside and around the corner of the barn. Adrian's barn was what they called a bank barn, meaning it was built into the side of a hill. The top portion of the barn could be driven into with a buggy, and hay or supplies could be easily off-loaded and stored. Farther in, it became a loft that overlooked the bottom portion of the structure.

When she climbed the hill toward where Triangle was apparently having the time of his life, what Grace saw there was something she'd remember for a very long time. Adrian was waving his arms, trying to drive the pygmy goats into the upper section of the barn. Triangle was barking and running in circles. Millie, the blind donkey, stood near Adrian, shadowing his every step. And Dolly the red-rumped parrot sat on the open barn door, squawking as if her voice would help the situation.

Adrian's mouth fell open when he saw her standing there.

"Grace, is everything…is everything okay?"

"*Ya*. Just came to visit."

"Visit?" He glanced at his goats, then back at her, apparently at a loss for what to say.

"What are you doing…with the goats?"

"Oh. These. My *bruder* came by, said I need to move

all my animals inside because the worst of the storm is coming."

"Worst?"

"*Ya*, and then he couldn't stay, so I've been moving—" Nelly the pygmy goat dashed past him, then stopped and cried out like a very unhappy child "—trying to move them inside."

"That explains the camel and llama in your barn." She set the thermos and lunch box under the roof hang. "Let me help."

They spent the next thirty minutes together herding goats. They'd manage to get two in and three more would slip out. At one point, they had seven of the eight goats inside the large barn door, and Nelly decided to dash through the middle and scatter everyone. The rain began to fall harder, and Adrian's expression changed from frustrated to desperate.

That look, the one that conveyed how much he loved his crazy collection of animals and how worried he was, convinced Grace they needed to try something different.

"I have an idea," she called out over the wind. She ran over to the lunch pail and pulled out the peanut butter bars, then held them out to Nelly, who immediately ran to where she was standing. But instead of giving the beast the treats, Grace held the bars above her head and walked backward into the barn. Nelly followed Grace, and the other goats followed Nelly.

Dolly flew inside, Triangle circled around behind the slowest goat, and Adrian grabbed her thermos and slammed the barn doors shut.

Grace crumbled up two of the bars and let the pieces fall to the floor. The goats surrounded her, nudging one another, completely focused on the food at her feet.

"You're beautiful. Did you know that?"

"Pardon?" She glanced up, and what she saw in his eyes raised a lump in her throat.

"You're beautiful."

"I'm muddy and wet. We both are." She reached up, found her *kapp* had slipped back, half off her head, and attempted to pull it forward. But her hair was soaked and the *kapp* was soaked, so she pulled it off and wrung the rain out of it. Looking again at Adrian, she shrugged. "Want a peanut butter bar?"

Five minutes later, they sat at the edge of the loft, feet dangling over. It was a funny view, looking down at Kendrick and Cinnamon. The goats, even Nelly, had finally collapsed onto the hay behind them. Dolly the parrot sat atop one of the higher bales of hay, preening herself. Triangle had curled into a ball and was watching them through half-closed eyes.

"Are your other birds going to be okay?"

"Sure. Dolly, she's just used to following me around."

"She's a *gut* bird."

"And beautiful." He nudged his shoulder against hers. "Like you."

"Are you comparing me to a parrot?" Grace laughed as she pulled her hair over her left shoulder and finger combed the braid out. How had she managed to get so wet?

"It's a compliment."

"One can hope."

"I meant what I said earlier about you being beautiful." Adrian laid a hand over his heart. "Honest."

"Adrian, are you trying to sweet talk me in order to get more peanut butter bars?" She pulled another out of the lunch pail and leaned back, holding it out of his reach.

Which caused Adrian to reach for it, and then they both fell over in the hay, laughing, and Triangle belly crawled closer to lick them on the face.

When she looked up at Adrian, he pushed the hair out of her eyes, then he did what she'd been dreaming about for days. He kissed her—softly at first and then more thoroughly. Grace felt her face flush, wondered if she had mud on her cheeks, then realized she didn't care about any of that. The only thing that mattered was Adrian's fingertips on her face, his lips on hers, his eyes drinking in the sight of her.

And in that moment, Grace did something she hadn't been able to do since the day she'd first learned that she was pregnant with Nicole.

She stopped being scared.

She let go of her regrets.

She allowed herself to be happy.

When Adrian pulled away and sat up, she opened her eyes, looked around, then also popped up beside him.

"What's happening?"

"I don't know." Adrian cocked his ear toward the roof. "I think it's here."

"What's here?"

"The worst part of the storm. The part my *bruder* warned me about."

The rain against the roof was setting up quite a ruckus, and the day outside had turned significantly darker. Funny that she hadn't noticed any of those things while Adrian was kissing her.

"Let's go check it out." He stood and reached for her hand.

Grace froze because it occurred to her that she was doing more than putting her hand in Adrian's. It seemed like she was finally stepping back into the stream of her life, the part that moved forward, the part that would keep her from being alone. Which was all something that up until now she'd dared only to dream of.

It was risky, she realized. She could get hurt again. She didn't believe that Adrian would hurt her. She thought the risk was worth taking.

Adrian stood, waiting, holding out his hand to Grace.

She seemed to hesitate, and he wondered if he'd gone too far. Perhaps he shouldn't have kissed her so boldly. But being around Grace and not kissing her seemed a terrible thing to ask of a guy.

Then Grace slid her hand into his, and she smiled, and something clicked inside of Adrian. Something that was missing had suddenly, undeniably been found as he pulled her to her feet.

The goats were no longer frantic. Even Nelly had calmed down. Hand-in-hand, Adrian and Grace made their way across the loft and down the stairs, into the main part of the barn, and over to the windows.

"Wow." Grace stepped closer and pressed her nose against the window. "That's a crazy amount of rain."

"Ya."

"Are we…are we okay here?"

"Oh, *ya*. This happened before, maybe a year ago. I guess it was when you were gone."

"Your property flooded?"

"Sort of. The barn is on enough of a rise that it doesn't easily take on water, but my *bruder* and I decided to cut some trenches around the barn to make it even more secure."

"I'd wondered about those." Grace again pressed her

nose against the window. "It's like there's a moat around your barn."

"Exactly. Timothy said that when considering your land, you have to think like water. Where do you want it to go? Where do you need it to go? And how can you get it there? We worked on those trenches for a few weeks, but as you can see, it was a *gut* idea. The heavier rain should push through in an hour or so."

"Should I be worried about Nicole or my parents?"

Adrian squeezed her hand. "Their place is a little higher than mine, but let's go and see."

He led her back upstairs and to a window that faced her parents' farm. Even through the darkness of the downpour they could see a single light in the kitchen window.

"See? One light means all is fine."

"You know the signal?" She turned and looked up, studying him. He wanted to kiss her again, but he stopped himself when she started laughing. "Of course you know the signal. My *mamm* probably made sure you knew about it the first week you moved here."

"Pretty much."

"We should put one light in the window here so they'll know we're okay."

They found an old battery-operated lantern on the shelf and put it in the window. One home assuring the other that all was fine. One group calling out to the other as if to say you aren't in this alone. And once again, Adrian realized that was what he wanted more than anything else. He wanted Grace right here, by his side, every single day. He wanted her and Nicole to be his family.

"Marry me."

"What?" They were sitting among the pygmy goats,

and she had Heidi in her lap. She'd been rubbing the goat's silky ear between her thumb and forefinger. Now she looked up, the expression on her face saying she must have misheard him.

"I love you, Grace. I know… I know things have been crazy the last few weeks. My *dat*'s illness sort of interrupted our courting, but I care about you…about you and Nicole. I want us to be a family."

"Adrian—"

His mouth went suddenly dry when he saw her hesitation, but he'd jumped into it now. There was no backing out, and he didn't want to. He wanted to move forward, into their future, not backward where they had been. So he reached for her hand. "You don't feel the same?"

"I do. I care about you. I care about you very much." She pulled her hand away and resumed petting Heidi. "But there are things…things you don't know about me. Things that I need to tell you because they might change how you feel."

"Then, tell me." He'd been sitting beside her, but now he scooted around in front, so they were knee to knee, so he could look her in the eye. "Tell me anything and everything, but I promise you that it will not change how I feel."

She pulled the goat closer, held it in her arms as if it could give her the courage that she needed, and in that moment, Adrian's heart broke for Grace. What had she been through that frightened her still? And did it have to do with Nicole?

"Nicole isn't my cousin's child."

"Oh." His mind tossed about in an attempt to respond to that. "A friend's? Because it doesn't matter to me. She's your family now, and I want you both to be my family."

"She's my *doschder*, Adrian."

"Of course she is." He felt his head nodding like a bobble head toy. "And I will treat her the same, too."

"Adrian, look at me."

He raised his eyes to hers and waited.

"Nicole is my *doschder*, my flesh and blood. I met a boy…an *Englisch* boy who was working on one of the farms." She bit her lip, glanced down at the goat, then back at Adrian. "I fancied myself in love and he said he cared about me, and I… Well, I made some foolish choices."

A tear slipped down her cheek. Adrian longed to brush it away, but he sensed that if he moved now Grace might run away, run out into the storm and not return. So he waited, though it took every ounce of willpower to do so.

And while he waited, several things slipped into place. He remembered the way that friends and family would look at him when he'd praise Grace for raising another's child. He thought of how Grace's parents doted on Nicole—on their granddaughter. He recalled the moments that he'd seen Grace and Nicole together and how he'd wondered that they favored one another so much. He thought of his *schweschder* warning him to not be didactic, to not judge.

Of course Nicole was Grace's *doschder*.

He'd been blind not to see it, and though it was a testament to her youth and immaturity that she had stepped outside the rules of their *Ordnung*, a wayward teenager wasn't who was sitting in front of him now. The woman he was weathering the current storm with was older, wiser and confident. She was also loving and kind.

"I don't regret my mistakes." She raised her chin defiantly, but her voice… Her voice remained a whisper.

"How can I regret those mistakes when the result is Nicole? I can't imagine my life without her."

"Of course you can't." He reached for her hand now, no longer worried about if he was being careful enough. He needed to assure her that this thing, this part of her past, didn't matter. "Nicole is a blessing, Grace...regardless the circumstances she was born under."

"Do you think so?"

"*Ya.* Of course. None of us are perfect." He rubbed his thumb over hers. "The fact that you made a mistake, that you misstepped... Well, it seems to me you paid for that with your time away. And now you're home, with your *doschder*, and I've fallen in love with you."

"What about what you said before, the afternoon that Nicole was attacked by the ants? You spoke quite strongly about not being a hypocrite, about not having a foot in both worlds."

He had said those things. He wanted to slap a palm to his forehead. How could he have been so coldhearted? How could he have been so sure?

"Because that's exactly what I did, Adrian. And if that makes you think less of me, then our being together can't possibly work."

"It doesn't make me think less of you. How could I ever think less of you?" He looked down, turned her hand over and ran a fingertip across her palm. Then he looked up at her and smiled. "What I said that afternoon, it only proves that I still don't know it all and that I can be wrong. Can you live with that?"

"Of course I can."

She struggled to her feet, and he popped up beside her. But instead of moving into his embrace, she paced away from him, walked back over to the window. The rain was lessening, and the sky had lightened up enough that he could look past her and see the swirling waters racing away from his barn.

"I can't... I can't have everyone believing that Nicole is my cousin. I need to make a confession in front of the church."

He was shaking his head before she finished speaking. "Bishop Luke won't require that. You weren't a member of the church when you became pregnant."

"You're right."

She turned toward him now, looked up into his eyes, and Adrian felt himself falling more thoroughly in love than he'd thought possible.

"Luke has already told me that it's something I don't have to do, but I *want* to do it. I'm tired of living under a pretense, a lie, really. I want people to know that Nicole is my *doschder*, and if that makes them think differently of me—"

"Of us, Grace. You're not in this alone anymore."

"Okay. If they think of us differently or treat us differently in any way—"

"Then it will be their loss."

He pulled her into his arms, kissed her gently and then held her. But Grace wasn't done yet.

"There's something else." She stepped away, pulled him toward a bench. "The reason I was so worried about the tours, about the *Englischers*, is that I'm worried Nicole's father will show up and want custody of her."

"Can he do that?"

"I don't know. I've been afraid to ask anyone."

Adrian ran a hand up and down his jawline. Then he snapped his fingers. "I've got it."

"You've got it?"

"George has an *Englisch* friend who is a lawyer. We'll go to town as soon as we can and ask his advice."

"I'm so afraid of losing my baby."

"You're not going to lose Nicole. You're a *gut mamm*. There's no reason to lose her. As far as her father… It's better that we know what the *Englisch* laws say. We don't want to live with this hanging over us. We don't want to live afraid of what might happen."

"You're right. I know you're right." She covered her face with her hands. "Every time I think of Nicole staying with someone else, with a virtual stranger, I feel sick."

"Hey." Adrian pulled her hands away from her face. "We're in this together, okay? And *Gotte* didn't bring us this far to leave us. He didn't bring you home and put the two of us in each other's paths if there wasn't a way forward. He didn't do all of that only to abandon us now. Right?"

"Yes. Yes, I think you're right. I hope you are."

"The important thing is that we'll go through this together, not just you and me and Nicole, but both of our families, too. We'll stand together, Grace. And we'll find a way through this."

She snuggled into his arms, and Adrian said a silent prayer of gratitude that *Gotte* had brought her into his life. Then he realized she still hadn't answered his question.

He held her at arm's length and asked again. "Do you love me, Grace?"

"I do." Tears shone in her eyes, but she was smiling.

"Will you marry me? Will you and your *doschder* be my family?"

"Yes. Yes, I'll marry you. Nicole and I will be your family."

Chapter Fourteen

The next day the storms had pushed through, and they were able to meet with George's friend, Jason Stromburgh. He seemed to enjoy being a small-town attorney, and he assured them that he could investigate Nicole's father. Finding Kolby would be the first hurdle. Depending on where he was and his response to initial inquiries, they'd decide together how to proceed.

Grace expected to be a bundle of nerves in the days that followed, but she wasn't. Somehow, knowing that she wasn't in this alone, that Adrian was at her side supporting her gave her the courage to believe in herself. She'd handled being alone and pregnant, she'd handled being a single mom, and now she would handle this. *Gotte* would give her the wisdom and strength that she needed. *Gotte* had given her Adrian and Nicole and *gut* parents. She could trust that He wouldn't desert her now.

Six days later, they once again were ushered into Jason Stromburgh's office. He was probably the same age as Grace's father, with gray hair and a slim build. Like the last time they'd visited his office, he was wearing blue jeans and a snap-button western shirt.

Grace and Adrian sat side by side, with Nicole on Grace's lap. Her baby was a little girl now, a staggering eighteen months old. The days and weeks and months had flown much faster than Grace had thought possible. Certainly it was time to move on from the shadow that Grace had allowed to color her world.

"Good to see you both again. I trust you are well."

They both nodded, and Nicole stuck her fingers in her mouth and buried her face in Grace's dress.

"I suppose you want to skip the chitchat and get right to it." The attorney had a single file centered on the desk in front of him. He opened it, read through the first sheet, then smiled up at them. "I think you're going to like what I found."

Grace couldn't imagine that. She couldn't imagine anything on that sheet of paper that would make her feel happy.

"The person that you thought was Grace's father doesn't exist."

"I don't understand." Grace glanced at Adrian, who also looked confused.

"Kolby Gibson doesn't exist. I checked with the ranch where he supposedly worked."

"I'm sure he did work there. We drove by a couple times. We even stopped in to pick up his pay once."

Stromburgh sat back and steepled his fingers. "Do you remember if he received a check or cash?"

"It was cash."

"Makes sense. Apparently the name he gave to his employer was Kolby Gibson, the same name he gave you. He also told you he was born in Indianapolis and that he was twenty-five years old, correct?"

"*Ya.*"

"There is no public record of a Kolby Gibson who was born in Indianapolis in 1996. I expanded the search by five years in both directions. All that inquiry yielded was one young man who was born in 2001, but he died in a traffic accident five years ago."

They all three looked at Nicole. The Kolby Gibson born in 2001 couldn't have been her father.

"*Nein.* That can't be him."

Stromburgh sat up straighter and closed the folder. "Look, I know you're trying to do the right thing here, but you've met your legal obligation. You've attempted to find Nicole's biological father. The fact that he was working under an alias and that the information he gave you can't be corroborated, it means you're off the hook."

"He can't…" Grace felt suddenly light-headed. Could it possibly be this simple? She looked at Stromburgh, who smiled and waited patiently. Then she glanced at Adrian, who had sat back and breathed out a deep sigh. Finally, she looked down at Nicole, kissed her on top of the head and found her voice. "You're saying he can't come back and ask for his parental rights?"

"No. I don't believe he can. After all, he deceived you, and he made no attempt to follow up after your relationship ended."

Stromburgh tapped his fingers against the desktop. "I admire your desire to pursue due diligence, Miss Troyer. We've done what we can, and you can rest assured that I have been thorough in my investigation. Now, I suggest you move on."

"Move on?"

"If I'm not mistaken, you two are…"

Grace blushed, but Adrian smiled as if he'd just been handed the gift of a lifetime.

"*Ya*. We plan to marry, but Grace wanted to take care of this first."

"Then, I wish you both the best." Stromburgh stood, walked around the desk and shook hands with Adrian and Grace.

Nicole had recovered from her shyness and held out her doll to the attorney, who declared it beautiful. They stopped at the front desk to pay their bill, which was a staggering one hundred twenty dollars for what amounted to less than two hours work. Grace would have gladly paid double that for the peace of mind that Stromburgh's investigation had given her. She counted out the bills—money from the tour groups—and attempted to keep from laughing.

They stepped out into a perfect August afternoon.

"Something funny?" Adrian cupped a hand around her elbow.

"I was just thinking that the tour money helped to pay for the lawyer."

"I've heard those tours can be a real financial blessing for folks willing to participate in them." He ran a hand up and down her arm, then reached for Nicole. "I'm wondering if my two favorite gals would enjoy some ice cream."

"*Ya*. I think ice cream would be perfect."

It was while they were sharing their cups of strawberry and vanilla with Nicole, sitting at a picnic table, that Grace seemed able to speak of what they were to do next.

"Should we talk to my parents first?"

"If that's what you want to do."

"Then yours."

"Okay." Adrian grinned and spooned some strawberry into Nicole's mouth. She made a grab for the spoon, so he let her have it and put a little of his ice cream into an extra cup he'd asked for.

Nicole was quite satisfied to whack the spoon into the cup and laugh, though very little ended up in her mouth.

"You're going to be a *gut dat*."

"I am?"

"Ya."

"More, Adrian. More."

They both stared at Nicole in surprise.

"She said my name right. I can't believe it."

Maybe it was the stress of the last week, but Grace finally lost it. She started laughing and had trouble stopping. She held her stomach and then put her hands to her cheeks to cool them. Adrian watched and waited, his eyes dancing in amusement. She shook her head, pulled in a deep breath and used her napkin to wipe the tears from her eyes.

"She thinks we're funny, Nicole. Can you believe that?"

"What's funny is that she finally…" Laughter threatened to bubble out again, but Grace stopped it by taking a big drink from the cup of water. "Nicole can finally say your name, but it won't be your name for long. Soon she'll be calling you Dat."

"Oh, *ya. Gut* point."

"Much easier to say."

"Has a nice ring to it, too."

As they cleaned up their table and Nicole's hands and face, then climbed back into Adrian's buggy, Grace's mood grew more somber. What she had to do next was something she'd both dreaded and longed to do for over two years. She was finally going to be honest with her parents. And they were going to listen, whether they wanted to hear what she had to say or not.

She could handle their disapproval, but she couldn't handle their not knowing the truth.

When they reached the house, Adrian put his hand on her arm. "I need to go and check on the animals, but I can come back if you like."

"*Nein.* I need to do this on my own."

"All right." He kissed her lips. "I'll be praying that they are receptive to what you have to say."

He hesitated, but then he pushed forward. "What happened to you, that part about Nicole's father lying about his name—"

"Everything. He lied about everything."

Adrian reached toward her, tucked a strand of hair behind her ear. "You didn't deserve that, Grace. Neither you nor Nicole deserve to be treated that way. You deserve to be cherished."

She nodded, tears threatening to fall. But she wasn't going to cry. She was done with crying. She was ready to own up to her past, because she knew with certainty that it was the only way to embrace her future.

She waited to speak with her parents until dinner was finished, the kitchen was cleaned and Nicole was tucked into bed. Her *dat* was perusing the *Budget*, and her *mamm* was knitting at her usual lightning speed when Grace walked into the living room and sat down across from them.

"I would like to speak with you both—if now is a *gut* time."

Her *dat* lowered his paper and, sensing the seriousness of the moment, folded it. Her *mamm* finished counting the row she was on, then pushed her knitting needles into the ball of yarn. It was a little disconcerting, having both of their attention so completely on her.

"Adrian and I have decided to marry." She wasn't sure why that popped out first, but her parents reacted quite enthusiastically—which was to say that her *dat* grinned broadly and her *mamm* rose to give her a hug.

"There's more."

"More?" Now her *dat* looked confused and a tiny bit worried.

"I didn't want our marriage to be built on deception, so I told him about Nicole being my *doschder*. I told him about Nicole's biological *dat*."

"We don't need to go into that, Grace…" Her *dat* reached for the paper, but Grace leaned forward and put her hand on top of his.

"You may not need to hear it, but I need to say it."

Now her *mamm* looked visibly upset. She kept eyeing her knitting as if it could save her. Grace had the urge to snatch it away and tuck it out of sight.

"I know that you've never asked, that you've never really wanted to hear the details." Neither parent interrupted her now. "But as I said, I need to tell you. Two years ago, I met a young man named Kolby Gibson—at least, that's what he said his name was."

"Why do we need to know this, dear?" Her *mamm* clutched her hands in her lap. "You know we love Nicole—we love you both."

Grace decided the best thing to do was just plow through. "It turns out Kolby Gibson was not his real name. Adrian and I went to an attorney to see if Kolby might have parental rights. He doesn't, because he was working under a false name. He was dating me under a false name. I don't even know who he was...or is."

Her *dat* harrumphed and her *mamm* tsk-tsked.

"The point is that I don't have to worry anymore about him showing up here, about him wanting custody of Nicole. I don't know why I thought he might, but it was just always there, lurking in the back of my mind. Now... now I'm at peace. Now Adrian and I can begin our life together on solid ground."

She waited—partially to catch her breath after such a long speech and partially to give her parents a chance to comment.

They didn't.

"I know I must have disappointed you terribly. I understand now that my actions must have hurt you, and I'm sorry for that." She brushed away a tear. She'd sworn she wouldn't cry, but there were times when her emotions didn't follow orders very well. "And I ask your forgiveness."

Her *dat* looked at her *mamm*, who put her hand over his and squeezed. That image of her hand on his, of the way they were looking at one another, told her how much she had hurt them. She'd thought the past two years were difficult for her, but now she realized how heavy the burden was that they had carried. She felt such grief for that, for what she'd put these two good people through, that it nearly pinned her to the chair.

It was with great effort that she stood, walked over to the coffee table sitting in front of them and perched on the edge of it.

"Can you forgive me?"

"Of course we forgive you, Grace." Her *dat* scooted forward, placed his hand on top of hers. "The more

important question—the question that your *mamm*
and I have prayed over since you first told us of the
pregnancy—is whether you've forgiven yourself."

Tears cascaded down her cheeks, and Grace made
no attempt to wipe them away. She realized as she sat
there, her parents waiting for her answer, that she *had*
forgiven herself—not all at once, not at any particular
moment, but day by day as she'd watched Nicole grow,
as she'd fallen in love with Adrian, as she'd found God's
grace in her prayers.

"*Ya.* I have."

"Then we are happy for you, and you and Adrian have
our blessing." Her *mamm* put her hand on top of Grace's
dat's, the same hand that sat on top of Grace's.

It was a moment that Grace would always remember, and one that would sustain her through the tough
days ahead.

"Things went well, then."

Adrian and Grace were watching Nicole run through
his group of goats. She wasn't really running. It was more
like lurching from goat to goat, but the goats didn't seem
to mind. They'd become quite accustomed to the little
girl with the golden curls.

"*Ya.* Better than I'd hoped."

"And it's *gut*—to have that off your chest."

"It is."

"So what's the *but*?"

Grace started to laugh. "You know me pretty well."

"I'm a quick study when it comes to someone I plan
to spend the rest of my life with."

"Okay. I'm worried about your parents."

"Don't be." Adrian wished he could fast-forward

through the next twelve hours, not because he was worried about the outcome but because he could see how much this pained Grace. He hated to think that anything he might say or do, anything his family might say or do could cause her such concern.

"At least it will be over tonight." Grace sighed dramatically, only she wasn't being dramatic.

She looked as if she was having trouble pulling in a full breath. Adrian rubbed her back in slow circles, as he'd seen her do with Nicole.

"They're excited that you and Nicole are coming for dinner, and I'm pretty sure they've guessed that we're going to announce our intentions to marry."

"The rest will be a surprise, though."

"Maybe not as much as you think." When Grace looked at him in surprise, he squeezed her hand, then nodded toward Nicole. "She looks more like you than you realize."

"True."

"And your leaving town suddenly, then returning with a child… Let's just say it doesn't take a genius to figure things out."

Grace leaned her shoulder against his. "Did you? Figure it out?"

Adrian laughed. "Nope. But now that I look back, when I would mention to my *bruder* or George or my parents how *wunderbaar* you were to raise someone else's child—"

"You did that?"

"Yes, I did, and they'd always give me a look."

"A look?"

"As if I was a bit slow. I didn't understand it then, but now, thinking back… Well, I suspect most everyone had guessed the truth except me."

Grace hopped up and began pacing back and forth in front of him.

"That's going to make it worse—that they already know. They're going to think of me as a liar. I obviously should have done this months ago when I first came home."

Nicole had plopped down on the ground and stuck her fingers in her mouth. Adrian recognized that look. She was sleepy and about to start crying. Best to intervene before she wound herself up. He was at her side in three long strides. When he picked her up, she slipped her arms around his neck and rested her head on his shoulder, and Adrian realized he was a goner. Not only did he love the beautiful woman standing in front of him but he would do absolutely anything for this child.

He walked back over to Grace, who was still worrying her *kapp* strings.

"The people who love you will not judge you, and the people who judge you are not the ones who love you."

"What does that mean?"

"It means that everything will be all right."

"Okay."

"Let's take this baby girl back to your parents' house so she can have her afternoon nap. Tonight's a big night for all of us."

The evening with Adrian's family went better than he could have hoped. They were barely in the door and seated around the kitchen table when Grace asked if she could speak.

Before she managed to gather her thoughts, Adrian cleared his throat, waited until he had everyone's attention and then he said, "Grace and I, we love each other, and we want to marry."

His parents broke into large smiles.

His youngest *schweschder*, Lydia, squealed in delight.

His older *schweschder* Beth reached over to hug Grace. Her husband congratulated them, and though her *bopplin* were too young to have any idea what was going on, they clapped their hands in delight. Nicole began to bang her spoon against the tray of the high chair they'd sat her in. It was plain as day that she wanted to join in on the celebration. Adrian wanted to enjoy the moment, but he realized that Grace wouldn't be able to do so until she'd had her say.

So he raised his hands, indicating he wasn't finished. "Grace would like to share something with you."

She took her time looking around the table at each person, but when she finally started talking, she addressed her words directly to his parents. "If I'm to be a part of your family, which I hope and pray I am, then I know I must do so honestly. Nicole isn't my cousin, she's my child. I… I met an *Englischer* before I moved away, and I fancied myself in love."

She glanced at Beth, then Adrian, then back to his parents, who were now listening intently. "My parents thought I should move to Ohio while I was pregnant, and then when I returned, everyone just assumed that Nicole was my cousin. I should have set them straight, though, from the beginning, and I'm sorry that I didn't. I'll make a confession at church Sunday, but before I do so publicly, I wanted to share the truth with you…in case it changes the way you feel about…about our marriage."

Adrian's parents shared a look, one he'd seen a thousand times growing up. He knew what it meant. They were on the same page. They'd already discussed the topic at hand. They'd simply been waiting. Now his *mamm* stood, walked around the table and squatted next to Grace's chair.

"We will be proud to have you as a part of our family, you and your *doschder*." Which was all she needed to say in order to lift the burden of worry off Grace's shoulders.

As his *mamm* and Grace hugged, his *dat* stood. "I'd like to pray over this fine meal and also ask a special blessing on these two new additions to our family."

Everyone quieted and bowed their heads, even Nicole, who carefully placed her hands palm to palm as Grace had taught her.

"Heavenly Father, we thank You for this *gut* food and for all of Your provisions. This night, we'd especially like to thank You for bringing Grace and her *doschder*, Nicole, into our family. We ask that You bless this union between Adrian and Grace, that You guide them in all things, and that Your loving arms remain around them through the many years they will share."

Amens resounded vigorously around the table, and then dishes were passed as everyone talked at once. When Grace passed the bowl of mashed potatoes to Adrian, she met his gaze. In that moment, Adrian understood that this was the one thing that had worried her the most. The confession at church would be difficult, but what she had longed for, what she had needed was the blessing of their families. She could handle whatever happened at church because she would have Adrian, his family and her family supporting her.

Adrian realized there would be times, like this dinner and like the church service the next day, when he wouldn't be able to take a difficult thing out of his *fraa*'s path. But he could walk that path with her, and he was determined to do so.

After dinner when they'd moved to the sitting room, Lydia admitted that she was thrilled. She'd grown quite attached to Nicole. Now, sitting on the floor with the child, she glanced up at Adrian and said, "Guess I won't be paid anymore for babysitting."

"And why is that?"

"Adrian! I don't want to be paid for watching my own niece."

"Huh." He rubbed a hand up and down his face as if he was in deep thought, then snapped his fingers. "Nicole's a bit easier to care for now. It wouldn't hurt for her to be at the dinners with us. Maybe you could keep an eye on Nicole and help with the tourists at the same time."

"I could do that."

"In which case, you'd need to be paid, same as anyone else who helps with the *Englisch* tours."

Lydia smiled and nodded, then said to Nicole, "Let's go see my room. When you come over to stay with us, you can sleep with me."

Nicole slipped her right hand in Lydia's and proceeded to chatter about the baby doll she clutched in her left. As they walked down the hall, Adrian could hear Lydia saying, "*Ya*. You're sure? That's *gut*, Nicole."

Grace smiled at him as he pulled her down on the sofa next to him.

His mother sat across from them, a small quilt that she'd been attaching the binding to in her hands. She didn't pick up her quilting needle, though. Instead, she beamed at Grace and Adrian. "I thought Adrian might never marry."

"Thanks, Mamm."

"And I couldn't ask for a better daughter-in-law, a better granddaughter, than you and Nicole."

Which was exactly what he'd known she would say.

Adrian's father immediately started talking about asking the bishop to schedule a workday to build a home on Adrian's farm. "Can't expect any granddaughter of mine to be raised in a barn." Which had caused everyone to laugh, and suddenly for a brief moment, Adrian entertained the notion that it might actually be that easy.

The moment didn't last long.

Adrian's *schweschder*, Beth, came to the doorway between the kitchen and the sitting room and asked Adrian for his help in the kitchen. Grace was talking wedding plans with his *mamm*, his *dat* had gone out to check on the horses, and Nicole was in the bedroom with Lydia. Adrian shrugged and followed Beth into the other room.

Beth pounced as soon as they were alone in the kitchen.

She'd never been particularly patient…or subtle. That wasn't Beth's way, which was one of the things he liked about her. But the look on her face had him worried. This couldn't be good.

"Can you talk her out of the confession thing? You said yourself that Luke won't require it."

"She's sure it's the right thing to do."

Beth dropped a dish into the soapy dishwater and set about scrubbing it a bit too vigorously. "I think it's a bad idea."

"Why?"

She slipped the plate in the rinse water. He plucked it out and dried it, then set it in the cabinet.

"Because people can be cruel, Adrian. It's your job to protect her from those people."

"Grace is a big girl. She has a mind of her own, and this is what she wants to do. She wants a fresh start—"

"It won't be a fresh start, though. Don't you see? When she first came back—" Beth glanced over her shoulder to confirm they were still alone, then lowered her voice "—some people, a few, were quite unkind about Grace and her situation."

"Ah. You're talking about the gossips in our community."

"It's taken six months for them to finally move on to someone else. This will just stir them up all over again."

"'Better to hold out a helping hand than to point a finger.'"

"Really?" She stopped scrubbing mid-plate. "You're quoting a proverb to me?"

He smiled and patted her clumsily on the shoulder. "I appreciate your concern, but Grace is right about this. I plan to stand beside her and support her, and I know you will, too. As to what other people do... We have no control over that."

She pointed a soapy finger at him. "Just remember I warned you."

"Duly noted."

He thought they were finished with the topic, then Beth added, "Grace will fit right into this family. Stubborn, like everyone else."

"Including you."

His sister mock scowled at him as he walked out of the kitchen. Adrian considered sharing his *schweschder*'s warning with Grace that night as he drove her back home, but he couldn't do it. She was so happy with his family's response to her confession and their announcement. He couldn't ruin this moment for her. Instead, he would pray that the people who Beth had spoken of would have a change of heart. And if they didn't, then he would do what he'd said he'd do.

He'd stand beside Grace.

Chapter Fifteen

The new-members' class had finished the week before, and the next Sunday, each participant was to be baptized. Grace had shared the details of her past with her bishop. He hadn't looked surprised, but he had assured her of *Gotte*'s promise to forgive all who repented.

"Do you repent your past misdeeds, Grace?"

"*Ya*, I do."

It had been as simple as that. It had always been that simple, only she hadn't been ready. Now she was.

She had asked for permission to address the congregation before her baptism, and Bishop Luke had agreed. He seemed to recognize that this was something she needed to do. He'd even given her a list of scripture to study. "And then if you still feel you should speak, of course you may."

Confess your faults one to another...

If we confess our sins, He is faithful and just to forgive us...

And were baptized of him in Jordan, confessing their sins.

Grace understood that by speaking the truth to her

family and Adrian's family and her bishop, she'd fulfilled her duty. But her heart needed to clean the slate. She'd lived under a false pretense for too long.

Sunday morning came, and she remained convinced that a confession was the proper thing to do, the thing she needed to do.

She barely heard the words of the sermon.

And though voices rose in song around her, she found that her mind couldn't focus on the lyrics.

So instead, she prayed, and she waited.

When finally the service was near its conclusion, Bishop Luke stood and addressed the group. As was typically the case, there were about three hundred people gathered on the benches that had been placed outside under the shade of the maple trees. This Sunday, they were at George and Becca Miller's farm, which helped to calm Grace's nerves. They were a kind family, and George had been a good friend to Adrian.

"Our new-member class concluded this week, and I'm happy to share with you that we have eight candidates for baptism."

There were murmurs of "Amen" and "Praise God" and "Hallelujah."

"Before we begin, Grace Troyer would like to share a few words."

It wasn't unheard of for a woman to speak in church. Contrary to what *Englischers* thought, women did have a voice in the workings of the congregation. However, it was unusual for a woman to formally address the entire group. Grace's *mamm* reached for Nicole, but Grace shook her head and carried her *doschder* with her to the front of the congregation.

"I want to thank you—my church family—for being

so kind to me and to my *doschder*, Nicole, since we have returned from Ohio."

There were many nods and smiles, but Grace knew this didn't mean they understood what she was saying. They considered Nicole her *doschder*, but they didn't yet understand that she was her *doschder*. She could have stopped there, but then it wouldn't be a confession. Would it? Grace swallowed, found Adrian's gaze from the men's side of the group and continued.

"Today, before I'm baptized, I want to confess that I stepped outside the lines of our *Ordnung* when I became pregnant with Nicole. I was a single woman, and Nicole's father was an *Englischer*. I should have controlled my emotions and my actions better. I should have acted in a manner that respected the way my parents raised me. My deeds and my words should have been above reproach."

Now she searched the crowd to find her *mamm* and then her *dat*. Her *schweschders* Georgia and Greta, were also there with their families. Technically, they belonged to another church community, but they'd wanted to be there for the celebration of Grace's baptism.

The group as a whole had gone suddenly quiet, as if they were waiting for Grace to offer a better explanation for her actions.

"Moreover, I should have been honest from the day I returned. I have prayed to *Gotte* and sought His forgiveness, and today, before my baptism, I ask for yours."

She noted one, two, maybe three people who refused to meet her gaze, but overall, there were many nods of approval.

Bishop Luke stepped forward. "Now if all the candidates will come to the front, we will celebrate the holy sacrament of baptism."

Grace's *mamm* hurried up to where Grace stood and took Nicole. Grace and the others who were to be baptized sat in chairs that the deacons had placed near the front.

One by one, Bishop Luke and George Miller moved down the row. When they came to Grace, she covered her face with one hand as she'd seen so many before her do. Luke had reminded them of the reason for doing so at their last meeting. *The covering of your face indicates submission and humility to the church.*

George Miller was one of the deacons. He held the bucket of water, which he ladled out into Luke's hands. The bishop poured the water from his hands over Grace's head. He did so once, twice and then a third time. As he did, he prayed for *Gotte*'s blessing on her life, her child and her future.

And in that moment, Grace finally felt cleansed.

She understood that the water wasn't special in and of itself. It was the fact that they were following Christ's example. She was ready to live her life that way—for Nicole, for Adrian and for herself. She was ready to live a life that she wouldn't have to apologize for.

The next hour passed in a blur, with members coming up and congratulating her. Many promised to pray for her and Nicole. Through it all, Adrian stood by her side. They'd decided to wait a month to announce their intention to marry, but it was plain to anyone with eyes to see that they were in love.

They sat with George and Becca as they ate. Together the four spoke of children, summer crops and their future plans.

Grace and Adrian planned to wed in the fall.

George and Becca were expecting their seventh child.

All four were looking forward to attending the summer festival at the park the next weekend. They made plans to meet up and go together.

So this is what it feels like to have friends.

The thought seemed ludicrous, even to Grace. George and Becca had been their friends before her confession. But their kindness touched her heart, as did the kindness of others.

One of the girls she'd attended school with walked up to Grace after she'd finished eating and invited her to attend a sew-in the following week.

"All the *mamms* are working on quilts for the auction for the schoolhouse," Anna Lapp explained. "Your Nicole will be attending before you know it."

She'd squeezed Grace's arm, then pulled her into a hug before hurrying off to stop her son from attempting to climb on top of one of George's goats.

Perhaps the other *mamms* never had excluded her.

Maybe Grace had excluded herself.

There were only three people who were rude to her. The first had confronted her when Adrian was standing by her side.

"It's easy to confess a thing, but it's another matter to change your ways," Widow Schwartz had muttered, shaking her head and walking away.

Adrian had pulled her closer to his side, but the widow's words hadn't wounded Grace as much as she had expected. She saw now that Widow Schwartz was simply lonely and perhaps hurting from some past experience that she'd never spoken of to others. Grace understood that sort of pain.

Donna and Meredith Bontrager had turned their backs and refused to speak when Grace and Adrian had put their dishes in the bucket of soapy water. Adrian had wanted to say something, but Grace had touched his arm and nodded toward where the children were playing. "Let's go check on Nicole."

So they had.

She saw no reason to let two bitter women ruin her day. Donna and Meredith had always been gossips. Grace had tried for months to ignore them and not allow their rudeness to sting. She understood now that it was possible she would always be the recipient of their gossip. So be it. She couldn't stop people from talking poorly of her, if they were so inclined.

The day had gone better than she'd hoped.

Most everyone was quite supportive, and the few who weren't kind at least were in the minority. Grace decided she could live with that.

It was while she was putting Nicole down for a nap on a blanket under the maple trees that Deborah King approached her. Grace took in a deep breath and squared her shoulders. Deborah was Georgia's sister-in-law. Grace's *schweschder* had shared once that certain members of the family were quite strict.

Perhaps if Nicole hadn't been lying there, listening with wide eyes, Grace would have ignored the woman's words. Of course Nicole couldn't understand what she was saying, but that wasn't the point to Grace. The point was that it was her job to protect Nicole.

She wasn't going to tolerate anyone being unkind to her *doschder*, and it was best to set people straight on that now. Anyone who thought they could be hurtful to Nicole would have to go through Grace to do so.

Deborah stopped directly in front of Grace, wagging her finger and frowning. "I would think that you'd have the sense to at least move somewhere else, if not for your own sake, for Nicole's."

Grace froze in the process of handing her daughter her favorite doll, a Plain doll with a lavender dress and white apron. She remembered sewing the clothes for the doll. The way that Nicole had smiled when she'd first showed her the matching dress. Now Nicole accepted the doll, clutched it to her chest and popped her two fingers into her mouth.

Grace stood, straightened her dress and then faced Deborah. "I will thank you to not speak unkindly in front of my *doschder*."

"I was merely being honest and saying what others are thinking."

"Others are welcome to share their concerns with me privately, as you should have done."

"Well, I never…"

"Never what, Deborah? Never made a mistake? Never regretted a moment of weakness? Never wished that you could go back and change something?" Grace's temper rarely flared, but it was in danger of igniting. She pulled in a cleansing breath and remembered Bishop Luke pouring water over her head. She remembered the commitment of her baptism. "The truth is that I wouldn't change that mistake I made—I will gladly carry the burden of the things I've done wrong—since it means I'll have the joy of Nicole in my life."

"Humph." Deborah pulled her purse string over her shoulder and strode away.

And instead of feeling slighted or hurt or sad, Grace had the urge to laugh. She turned back to her baby girl, who pulled her fingers out of her mouth long enough to point and declare, "Adrian."

Grace turned and saw the man she loved walking toward her. She felt the sun's rays on her skin, but it was what was in her heart that sent warmth through her. She'd faced the very worst that could happen, and put it behind her.

Her heart felt lighter, so much lighter.

As Adrian sat beside her on the quilt, she forgot about Widow Schwartz and Donna and Meredith. Instead, she let her thoughts drift over the people who had been kind, over her family and Adrian's.

Gotte had provided them with the people they needed.

All that was left was to walk together into the future that was waiting just over the horizon.

Epilogue

Grace heard the delivery truck pull into their drive. She was moving more slowly these days. Her second child was due in two weeks. By the time she made it to the front porch, the delivery man was pulling away down the lane.

But the box of books were there.

Adrian must have heard the truck, or perhaps he was sticking closer to the house these days. He was certain their child would be born early. "Eager to meet everyone," he'd said the night before. "Especially his big sister."

Which had started Nicole asking a dozen questions.

Would she be able to play with him or her?

Could they share a room?

How did the baby come out?

Would it be like the kittens in the barn?

Nicole had turned four, and questions were her favorite thing.

Adrian scooped Nicole up in his arms and hurried toward the front porch.

"The books?"

"*Ya.*"

"Here. Use my pocket knife." He opened the small knife and handed it to her, handle first. "Careful."

"Of course." She slit the top of the box and let out a small gasp when she saw the covers. She'd seen them before, pictures of them, but this was the first time she'd held a copy.

Plain & Simple Recipes
By Grace Schrock

The front cover showed a picture of their garden, with Nicole squatting and picking cherry tomatoes from a plant. Only the back of her *kapp* and dress showed, and her little hand reaching for the tomatoes. Peeking out of the corner of the cover was Kendrick the Llama—as usual, he was poking his head where it didn't belong.

"It's a beautiful book. I'm so proud of you."

"Pride is a sin," Grace murmured.

"As you're aware, I'm not a perfect man."

"Walk with me to *Mamm*'s?"

"Of course."

Grace tucked one of the copies under her arm, and the three of them walked down the drive, down the lane and next door to her parents'.

Grace remembered returning there when Nicole was just a babe. So much had happened since then—the tours, falling in love with Adrian, sharing the truth about Nicole.

Their marriage.

A new home built by their church community.

The last two years hadn't all been rosy. Adrian's *mamm* had suffered a stroke and died a year after they wed.

A tornado had come through the year after that and taken several neighbors' barns.

But those things had brought them closer together. They were a family, and Grace was so grateful for that. They had each another to depend on through the trials and tribulations, and of course, the joys of life. The baby inside her moved, and she covered her belly with her hand.

"Everything okay?" Adrian's voice was low and close to her ear.

Nicole had stopped to pick a yellow flower. Yellow was still her favorite color.

"Everything is *wunderbaar.*" She kissed her husband, then slipped her hand in his. As she did, she thanked *Gotte* for how far He'd brought her, for the way He had knit this family together, for His care and provision. She knew that was one thing she could always depend on— *Gotte*'s provision. No matter what lay ahead, she didn't need to be afraid.

* * * * *

If you loved this story,
pick up the other books in the
Indiana Amish Brides series,

A Widow's Hope
Amish Christmas Memories
A Perfect Amish Match
The Amish Christmas Matchmaker
An Unlikely Amish Match
The Amish Christmas Secret

from bestselling author
Vannetta Chapman

Available now from Love Inspired!
Find more great reads at www.LoveInspired.com

Chicken Divan Casserole

A Plain & Simple Recipe

1 cup uncooked rice
1 cup diced carrots
4 boneless, skinless chicken breasts
2 tablespoons butter
3 tablespoons all-purpose flour
Salt and pepper to taste
1 cup chicken broth
½ cup milk or half-and-half
¼ cup + 2 tablespoons Parmesan cheese, divided
1 pound frozen broccoli florets

1. Preheat oven to 350 degrees and lightly grease a 12 x 8 inch baking dish.
2. Prepare rice according to package, stir in carrots and spread mixture into prepared baking dish.
3. Spray large skillet with cooking spray. Heat over medium-high heat. Brown chicken breasts 2 minutes on each side. Arrange over rice.
4. To prepare sauce, melt butter in saucepan. Whisk

in flour, salt and pepper. Cook and stir 1 minute. Gradually whisk in broth and milk. Cook and stir to boil. Reduce heat and simmer 2 minutes. Remove from heat and stir in 1/4 cup cheese.

5. Arrange broccoli around chicken. Pour sauce over top. Sprinkle remaining 2 tablespoons Parmesan cheese over chicken.

6. Cover with foil and bake 30 minutes. Remove foil and bake additional 10-15 minutes. Broil for 2 minutes if crispy chicken is desired.

Makes 6 servings

Dear Reader,

Have you ever regretted a past decision?

Grace Troyer regrets the casual relationship that resulted in her pregnancy and subsequent banishment to Ohio. But she doesn't regret the blond-haired daughter who brings joy to every day of her life.

Adrian Schrock thinks he is happy raising exotic animals and conducting *Englisch* tours. In Adrian's life, things are black-and-white—his opinion of how the world works is simple and clear. Knowing this about him, Grace doesn't think he'll be able to digest the truth of her situation and still care for her.

But people can change. Grace is more mature than the young woman who too easily fell in love and lost her way. And the depth of Adrian's feelings for her are stronger than his beliefs about the world. If it means that he must learn to see that some things aren't simple and clear, that some things are quite complicated, then he's willing to do that.

I hope you enjoyed reading *The Baby Next Door*. I welcome comments and letters at vannettachapman@gmail.com.

May we continue to "always give thanks to God the Father for everything, in the name of our Lord Jesus Christ" (*Ephesians* 5:20).

Blessings,
Vannetta

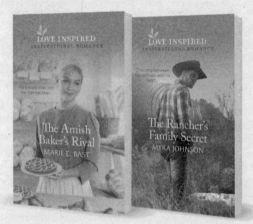

*Arleta Bontrager's convinced no Amish man will
marry her after she got a tattoo while on* rumspringa,
*so she needs money to get it removed. But taking a job
caring for Noah Lehman's sick grandmother means
risking losing her heart to a man who has his own
secrets. Can they trust each other with the truth?*

Read on for a sneak preview of
Hiding Her Amish Secret,
the first book in Carrie Lighte's new miniseries,
The Amish of New Hope.

Arleta had tossed and turned all night ruminating over Sovilla's
and Noah's remarks. And in the wee hours of the morning, she'd
come to the decision that—as disappointing as it would be—if
they wanted her to leave, she'd make her departure as easy and
amicable for them as she could.

"Your *groossmammi* is tiring of me—that's why she wanted
me to go to the frolic," she said to Noah. "She said she wanted to
be alone. And if I'm not at the *haus*, I can't be of any help to her,
which means you're wasting your money paying me. Besides, her
health is improving now and you probably don't need someone
here full-time."

"Whoa!" Noah commanded the horse to stop on the shoulder
of the road. He pushed his hat back and peered intently at Arleta.
"I'm sorry that what I said last night didn't reflect the depth of my
appreciation for all that you've done. But I consider your presence
in our home to be a gift from *Gott*. It's invaluable. Please don't
leave because of something *dumm* I said that I didn't mean. I was
overly tired and irritated at—at one of my coworkers and... Well,
there's no excuse. Please just forgive me—and don't leave."

Hearing Noah's compliment made Arleta feel as if she'd just
swallowed a cupful of sunshine; it filled her with warmth from

her cheeks to her toes. But as much as she treasured his words, she doubted Sovilla felt the same way. "I've enjoyed being at your *haus*, too. But your *groossmammi*—"

"She said something she didn't mean, too. Or she didn't mean it the way you took it. If I know my *groossmammi* as well as I think I do, she felt like you should go out and socialize once in a while instead of staying with her all the time. But she knew you'd resist it if she said that, so she turned the tables and claimed she wanted the *haus* to herself for a while."

That thought had occurred to Arleta, too. "*Jah*, perhaps."

"I'm sure of it. I can talk to her about it when—"

"*Neh*, please don't. I don't want to turn a molehill into a mountain." Arleta realized she should have spoken with Noah before jumping to the conclusion that neither he nor Sovilla wanted her to stay. But she'd been so homesick yesterday, and she'd felt even more alone after she'd listened to the other women implying how disgraceful it was for a young woman to work out. Hannah's lukewarm invitation to the frolic contributed to her loneliness, too. So by the time Sovilla and Noah made their remarks, Arleta already felt as if no one truly wanted her around and she jumped to the conclusion they would have preferred to employ someone else. She felt too silly to explain all of that to Noah now, so she simply said, "I shouldn't have been so sensitive."

"*Neh*. My *groossmammi* and I shouldn't have been so insensitive." Noah's chocolate-colored eyes conveyed the sincerity of his words. "It can't be easy trying to please both of us at the same time."

Arleta laughed. Since she couldn't deny it, she said, "It might not always be easy, but it's always interesting."

"Interesting enough to stay for the rest of the summer?"

Don't miss
Hiding Her Amish Secret *by Carrie Lighte,*
available May 2021 wherever
Love Inspired books and ebooks are sold.

LoveInspired.com